I0748495

BINGO, BANGO, MYSTERY

KEVIN DOG

BLASTER BOOKS

Copyright © 2025 by Kevin Dog

All rights reserved. No part of this publication may be reproduced, stored, or transmitted in any form or by any means, electronic, mechanical, photocopying, recording, scanning, or otherwise without written permission from the publisher. It is illegal to copy this book, post it to a website, or distribute it by any other means without permission.

No portion of this book may be reproduced in any form without written permission from the publisher or author, except as permitted by U.S. copyright law.

This novel is entirely a work of fiction. The names, characters, and incidents portrayed in it are the work of the author's imagination. Any resemblance to actual persons, living or dead, events or localities is entirely coincidental.

Kevin Dog asserts the moral right to be identified as the author of this work.

Hardcover ISBN: 978-1-7328857-2-1

Edited by Christine Barker

Cover by Ember East

For my favorite mystery authors...
Agatha Christie, MK Dean, and J.C. Fuller

CONTENTS

ONE

As I glanced around the Bingo Haven, I saw all of the usual players, and my eyes couldn't help but be competitive even at my older age. I had just retired from my career as the local librarian, and sometimes, I couldn't help but think that I missed my calling as a professional bingo player. I laughed to myself, but something caught me off guard. I saw Ruby Siren, the Bingo Haven manager, arguing with another patron from the hall.

I tried not to pay too much attention to this small detail, but my instincts were taking over, and I knew something wasn't right.

"Bingo!" Jeannine shouted from beside me.

I looked back down at my seven cards, and I hadn't been paying attention, or I would have shouted bingo two numbers ago. Drat. I'll just need to be more careful. I looked over my shoulder and tried to follow Ruby's figure until she was entirely out of my sight. Something still wasn't sitting right in the pit of my stomach.

"Time for new cards," the announcer called.

I got up from my spot, handed my cards in, and paid for another around when I saw the arguer standing right beside me. He wore a pained expression, and when he looked up, I couldn't help but notice the frustration that he wore on his body features. He quickly tried to hide it under a mask of happiness, but I was able to see right through it.

"I haven't seen you around lately?" I asked him.

"Oh, Lola. I've been over at the other Bingo Hall, you know, Vixen's Bingo Palace?" he replied.

"Right, Tom," I said as I finally remembered his name.

"Do you mind if I sit next to you?" he asked.

"Not at all,"

We both walked over to where I had been sitting and as we placed our cards on the table, we sat in companionable silence. I was about to call out my Bingo when Tom received a call on his cell phone.

"Hello?" he answered as he got up from the table so as not to be rude.

Drat. I really needed to pay better attention to my surroundings. I was about to call it a day when I couldn't help myself, but I looked over at my partner's cards, and he didn't mark a single number. I could have sworn that I saw him tabbing at the numbers just as I had been, except there was something different about his cards.

"All right, time to turn your cards in," the announcer said.

I wasn't ready to give these over yet because it looked like some sort of coded message. I looked back over to the employee-only door, but Tom hadn't yet come out. I flipped his cards over, and there was writing on one of the cards. I examined it closer, and it was a note written for me.

Dear Lola, don't believe anyone within the halls of the Bingo World.

I grabbed the card with my hidden note written on it and tucked it away inside my purse before anyone could see anything. I got up from my seat and turned in all of my cards along with Tom's, and I was heading toward the employee doors to ask a slew of questions.

A female's scream radiated throughout the entire Bingo Haven's walls, and I could tell it was coming from the doors I was about to bombard. I couldn't help myself, but I rushed over and burst through the door, and what I saw was Tom lying down on the floor, dead.

I placed my hand over my mouth to stifle a gasp when my dear friend Jasper ran up behind me.

"I was about to leave when I heard the commotion," Jasper said.

I turned around and tried to wipe the scene that I had just witnessed away from my memory.

"Call the Police," was all I was able to get out as I walked away from the crime scene.

I pulled a chair up and sat down, when I couldn't help but to notice that there was a bloody footprint on the floor just outside of the employee-doors.

"Wait!" I said as I jumped up, and rushed over to the evidence.

I quickly began to take pictures of the print, and I was completely flabbergasted as to why or how we hadn't destroyed it.

"Yes, I need the Police. There has been a murder at the Bingo Haven in Greenfield." Jasper's voice rang through the area.

I peeked up from what I was doing, and I began to survey the area. What I saw caught me off guard. I watched as Ruby was having a heated argument with Victoria Smith, the owner of Vixen's Bingo Palace.

I watched as four minutes ticked by on my watch when the Police arrived.

"Ma'am, please step away from the crime scene," an unfamiliar officer said to me.

"Easy, Franks," Officer James said.

"Officer James, I was trying to preserve the crime scene because we almost messed up this bloodied boot print," I said to them.

"Thank you, Lola, for trying to preserve the crime scene, but we'll take it from here," Officer James ordered.

"Who was the last person to have seen our victim alive?" Officer Franks asked.

"I was," I said, as I slowly began to get off of the dirty floor and back away from the fresh bloody evidence.

"You also thought it was wise to try and *preserve the evidence*?" Officer Franks said with an accusing tone.

"Listen, Officer, I was the last to see him alive because he was sitting next to me at the tables during the last round being called," I said.

"Alright, the both of ya," Officer James paused as though he was thinking the best way to handle the situation. "Lola, I'm going to need to talk with you first. Nobody can leave the area until they have had their interview with an Officer,"

I allowed Officer James to lead me away from the evidence and anybody else with whom I could have possibly collaborated a story with. We walked over to an empty table, and everybody gave us our space so we could have as much of a private conversation as we were going to get. He pulled out a chair for me, and I gladly accepted it. He walked behind me to get to the other side of the table; that way, we faced each other.

"Miss. Lola LaRue, can you describe the events leading up to the death of Mr. Thomas Burchfield?"

I began to describe what I had seen, leaving out the details of the letter I had picked up and put in my purse.

"That's everything pertinent that I saw," I finished.

"Can you tell it to me again?" he questioned.

I went over my story two more times, totaling three altogether.

"Am I finished?"

"For now. Please go home and don't leave town in case we need to get ahold of you again. Do you still live in the same place?"

"Yes, the same place I would walk from every time you needed help with a book report that nobody else could assist you with," I remarked.

"Please be careful," he said with a broad smile.

I got up from my seat, grabbed my purse, and walked out of the Bingo Haven. I usually walked if my destination wasn't too far, but today, I had decided to drive. As I got into my car, I put my purse in the passenger seat, started my old sedan, put the car in gear, and drove out of the parking lot.

There was too much on my mind, and I wanted to go home to work some things out. As I drove toward my destination, I couldn't wait to get into my family-owned house.

As I walked in, I immediately went to go sit in my favorite cream-colored chair, not bothering to put my purse in its usual spot. I sat down and heaved a sigh from what I had seen today.

Upon looking around my living room, I saw all of the memories that were made in or around my home. My wondrous life as a librarian made it easy to connect with the locals here in town; I would help kids with their book reports or simply help new or veteran mothers find bedtime stories for their little ones. Even fathers would come in and ask if any new books had arrived yet so they could read them during their nighttime lullabies. The pictures from my retirement party were currently still sitting out on the counter where I was working on scrapbooking them.

My siamese cat jumped in my lap as I picked up the daily crossword puzzle. I stared at it blankly and began to pet my cat without noticing what was really going on in my mind. I sat for almost an hour with her on top of me before she finally yawned and stretched before getting down. The day that I found her as a stray always clung to my mind. It took the stray cat quite sometime before she trusted me, but we came to a mutual agreement about the food, and when she did trust me enough, I brought her into my home.

I looked back down at the crossword, and I realized that I hadn't even started when the doorbell sounded. I got up from my chair, and before I could get to the door, someone began banging on it very loudly.

"Just a moment!" I shouted.

"Lola!" Jasper's voice was muffled as it came through the door.

"Oh, Jasper, it's only you. Come on in," I replied.

The door suddenly opened, and there stood my partner in crime, and the look on his face was something that I had seen before.

"Lola, what about if we..." he trailed.

"Don't even think about it," I interrupted him.

I walked away from the door and back toward the living room. Jasper was right on my heels.

"Think about it; with your memory and cunning wit, we could be major players in the case," he pleaded.

I sat back down in my chair, and Jinx, my cat, was about to jump back into my lap until Jasper sat in one of the chairs opposite of me. She always favored him, and I knew deep down that he always had good intentions, no matter how crazy they sounded.

"How are we going to get any of the information needed?" I questioned.

"We could always go back to the scene?" he wagged his eyebrows.

"We just left, wouldn't that look suspicious?" I asked.

"Yes, but we can go back tomorrow because they can't close the business down, and with my knowledge of the inner workings systems of the hall and your brilliant brain, we could scope out all of the facts that are needed," Jasper trailed on.

I contemplated what he said and a sudden thought occurred to me.

"What if we go to Vixen's Bingo Palace instead?"

"Why would we go there?"

"Ruby and Victoria were having an argument right as the Police showed up, we might be able to get some information from some of the other patrons," I said.

"I love the way you think,"

"You drive," I said as I got up and went to grab my purse.

We both went to his truck; I stepped onto the sideboards, climbed into the passenger seat, waited for him to start the giant machine, and headed to the rival bingo hall. Once we were on the road, it took us no time at all to get to Vixen's Bingo Palace.

TWO

I hardly ever went to the Vixen Palace due to the cheap prizes, higher rates, and the fact that you could only have three cards at a time. What a shame, I always thought.

When the two of us entered, it looked the same, except almost everybody from the other hall had ventured over here. This place always reminded me of a casino, with its flashing lights and overly hyped promotions.

"To what do I owe this pleasure?" A familiar voice asked.

As Jasper and I stepped through the doors, the owner of the Vixen Hall greeted us. I could feel the tension in the air, knowing that we were not exactly her favorite patrons.

"Ah, lady Victoria," Jasper said.

"Did you finally come to take me up on my offer about working here?" she asked as she crossed her arms and cocked an eyebrow.

"You know, I think that I'm going to head over and buy a round of cards," I said.

"Zip it, Lola," Victoria bit out.

"Ladies, there is no need for any hostility," Jasper butted in.

I didn't dare say another word as I began to walk away from her.

This was her establishment, after all, but that was no way to treat a paying customer.

"I can tell that you're not here to take me up on my offer; what is it that you want?" I overheard her asking Jasper.

"To take a tour of your fine establishment..." his voice trailed on.

I walked away from him and his assignment and began my own investigation from the others that had filled the usual barren hall. As I gazed around, I couldn't help but notice that almost everybody from the other hall was here. It was as if they weren't going to let the idea of being suspects in the ongoing murder investigation stop their addiction.

I walked over to the card keeper and bought a single round with the max card count of three, and I heard whispers coming from behind me.

"I think she did it," one whispered voice said.

"She was the first to be interviewed," another said a little louder.

So, they all knew that I had been the second on the scene, and I could tell that everybody here thought that I was the killer. I thanked the card keeper and walked away to sit at a barren spot so I could overhear many conversations without being suspicious.

I set my cards and my purse down on the table, and Jasper walked out onto the stage. There were many claps and shouts as though this was an award show.

"Thank you, fellow bingo lovers. I will put the rumors to rest that our dear friend, Lola, did not commit that heinous crime that we were all interviewed about earlier this morning." Jasper's voice trailed on.

I couldn't completely understand every word that he had been saying because a single person had gotten up from their seated position in the front row and walked back to me. They sat down without any cards, and this young man was probably in his early thirties. There were no distinguishing features about him, and if the Police asked me to pick him out of a lineup, I wouldn't have been able to.

"Is there something that I can help you with?" I asked as I stared into his green eyes.

"No, but I can help you," the stranger replied. "You're investigation, of course,"

"What makes you think that I'm running an investigation?"

"I saw the way you made sure nobody smudged the bloody footprint at the crime scene. I have my own personal lab that routinely runs evidence through it, and I can say for a fact that you missed something,"

"To my defense, I didn't have time to fully investigate,"

"I've seen the case files, Ms. Lola. Also, my lab has tested a few pieces of evidence already. There was a fiber and a torn article of clothing left at the crime scene."

"Why are you telling me this? Doesn't it break all the credibility of your lab?"

"Leave that to me," the stranger said, his determination evident in his voice.

The stranger got up and walked away without saying another word. I wasn't listening to Jasper as he had been calling out the numbers, but what the stranger said had my neurons firing, and I couldn't help but to think about a few things. I really needed to get back to that crime scene. There was just one problem. Everybody here already thought that I was the criminal in this crime; do the Police think so, too?

"Bingo!" someone shouted.

I gathered my empty cards, and after listening to a few more rumors about myself, I decided that I had heard enough for the day.

"Jasper?" I called out to my friend.

"Lola? Where did you go?" he cried out.

I walked over to him and nudged on his arm, signaling that I was ready to leave. I thought we were going to make it out scotch-free until Victoria stopped us again.

"Like what you saw?" she purred.

"It was impressive, I will consider your offer and get back with you," Jasper replied.

"Thank you for allowing me to play a round," I said.

"It's no problem. Nothing like free publicity," she cooed.

"What do you mean?" I asked.

"Oh, you know. Local Librarian turned murderer. It will drive the business through the roof," she sang.

"Let's go, Jasper," I said.

I pulled on his arm harder this time, not allowing anybody else to stop us before we got to his truck.

"Is everything alright?" he asked as he unlocked the doors.

"No,"

"I heard the rumors just as you did,"

"They are ugly rumors," I said through bitten-back tears.

"Lola, you are the strongest-willed person alive. Don't let the ugly lies cloud your judgment," Jasper said quietly.

"Will you please take me back to my house?" I asked in a quiet voice.

"Of course,"

I climbed back into his truck and allowed for my best friend to take me back to the house. When we pulled into the driveway, there were Police Officers already waiting for me.

"Oh great," I whispered.

Officer Franks stepped off of my front step and began to walk closer to Jasper's truck with his hand on his hip.

"Lola, come out of the vehicle with your hands up," he shouted.

"Oh, this is ridiculous," I shouted.

"Hands up!" Officer Franks shouted again.

"I can't get out unless I climb, and I need my hands to do that," I shouted as I opened the passenger door.

"Franks, stand down. She's not going anywhere," Officer James said.

"Officer James, what have I done?" I asked.

"Ms. Lola, we need to take you down to the station," Officer James replied.

"All you had to do was ask, not shout at me like a buffoon," I muttered.

"Franks, you really need to work on those people skills," Officer James said to his partner.

"Would it be ok if I drove down there instead of being in the back of a Police car?" I questioned.

"I'll take her down personally," Jasper volunteered.

"We'll follow you there. Just in case the two of you get any ideas," Officer Franks said.

"Franks! Seriously! Those people skills," Officer James said.

I shut the door to Jasper's truck, and we pulled out of my driveway and back into town, headed for the Police station.

"What are you going to do? Get a lawyer?" Jasper asked.

"For what? I didn't do anything?"

"The Police obviously think that you did,"

"I wonder if that was what the stranger at the Vixen Palace was talking about? He said that his lab already processed some evidence from the crime scene," I pondered out loud.

"The man sitting next to you?"

"Yes..." I trailed off as we entered the parking lot to the Police Station.

Jasper parked his truck, and Officer Franks came over to open the passenger side door. His head had been bowed slightly as though he had just been given a tongue-lashing. I underestimated Officer James.

Jasper had just rolled the window down so we could talk freely to the Officers.

"Please, come inside," Officer Franks asked.

"I can wait if you would like?" Jasper asked.

"Thank you, but that won't be necessary. We'll give her a ride back to her place when we're done," Officer James said as he walked over to assist me out of the vehicle.

Jasper parked his truck, and Officer Franks came over to open the passenger side door. His head had been bowed slightly as though he had just been given a tongue-lashing. I underestimated Officer James.

"Please, come inside," Officer Franks asked.

"I can wait if you would like?" Jasper asked.

"Thank you, but that won't be necessary. We'll give her a ride back to her place when we're done," Officer James said as he walked over to assist me out of the vehicle.

Jasper didn't even get the chance to cut the engine because both Officers assisted me in getting out of the truck. It made me feel older than I really was, but I wasn't going to knock on their mannerisms. Officer James had dismissed Jasper one final time by shutting the truck door. As the three of us began to walk away from the parking lot, I heard a sudden storm beginning to roar in the distance.

"Can we hurry inside?" I asked.

"Afraid that you will get wet?" Officer James asked.

"No, worse, melt," I laughed.

We walked at a slightly quicker pace toward the internal working system of the Police Station. My presence immediately caused tension in the room because everybody had stopped what they were doing. They all turned their attention in my direction, making me feel uneasy. I saw a pegboard with several pieces of evidence and my picture was attached onto the board with the main suspect written above it.

"Not even trying to hide it, are you?" I asked with sadness in my voice.

"I didn't even think about it," Officer James said as he realized I had seen my own image on the lead suspect list.

"I didn't do it," I said softly.

"Let's wait until we get into the interrogation room," Officer Franks said.

"Fine with me,"

I allowed both of them to walk me to the interrogation room, and what I found was no surprise. It was exactly like the TV shows. The room was cold, and everything inside was very meticulous, including the table with the pipe-like bar that held the handcuffed prisoners.

"Am I going to need to?" Officer Franks asked without finishing the sentence.

"People skills, Franks. She's not going anywhere and certainly not a threat to us," Officer James said.

Both Officers glanced at one another, but Officer James' face softened after a few moments as though his heart was breaking.

"Lola, can you tell me why your DNA was found at the scene?" Officer James asked.

"Yes, I can, as a matter of fact. I had been leaning over the bloody footprint, and nobody even asked for a sample of my DNA to exclude me,"

"It's hard to exclude a main suspect," Officer Franks butted in.

"How exactly do you expect me to clear myself?"

"Let's go over what happened one more time," Officer James said softly.

"No. We did this at the scene already, and the reason my DNA is at the footprint was because I was trying to ensure that the integrity of the crimescene was being contained. I hadn't seen the footprints when I first went into the room, but when I did see it, I wanted to ensure that nobody was going to step in it and ruin it," I said, crossing my arms as I sat back in the cold chair.

"Did you ever think to look at the rivalry between the two bingo halls?" Jasper's voice sounded into the room.

"Jasper? How did you get back here?" Officer Franks asked.

"I've got friends in high places," Jasper laughed into the intercom system.

With all of the concentration back on me a sudden thought dawned on me.

"Do I need a lawyer?" I asked as sadness crept into my voice.

"Innocent people don't need lawyers," Officer Franks said.

"They do if they are being framed for murder," I replied.

"Just a moment before we talk about getting a lawyer. What do you mean there is a huge rivalry between the bingo halls? I mean, I understand there's rivalry between the two businesses because they are the same type of business in one town, but is there really that much animosity between the two?" Officer James asked.

"Yes, both the manager of the Bingo Haven and the owner of Vixen Bingo Palace were seen arguing moments before the fateful accident," Jasper said into the intercom.

"Thanks, Jasper will take it from here," Officer James replied.

I couldn't help but roll my eyes, but Jasper was correct. The two had been seen at the bingo halls and were constantly going at one another.

"What evidence do you have on me?" I asked

"A strand of your hair was inside the bloody footprint," Officer Franks said.

"Of course, you would have found hairs that were mine. I already said I was trying to ensure the integrity of the evidence." I said half-annoyed.

"What if we give you the benefit of the doubt?" Officer James asked.

"What?" Officer Franks asked, stunned.

THREE

"I'm glad that you want to give me the benefit of the doubt, but what made you change your mind? Especially so quickly?" I asked.

"I remember when I was a child, and we were working so hard on that report about trains that you took the time to ensure that I had every piece of information that I was going to need to get an A on that report. Do you remember?" Officer James asked.

"I do. You were such a charming young man," I replied.

"I don't understand how someone who spent hours scouring research with me could do such a heinous crime. You even came to my house on multiple occasions to make sure that I had all of my reading material for any test,"

"So?" Officer Franks said.

"What I'm saying is that she went above and beyond every time anybody has asked her to do something. You think that a leopard can change its spots?" Officer James asked.

I looked in Officer Franks direction and saw that he had rolled his eyes but believed in his partner.

"So, what next?" he asked.

"Now, we get to do what I've always wanted to do. I'll be the outside party consultant," I said with a sense of purpose and excitement.

I stole a glance in Officer James' direction, and he wore the biggest smile, just like when he was a child. Both men got up from the table and exited the interrogation room.

"I think they like you," Jasper's voice rang through the intercom again.

I chuckled at the thought, but I was determined to get my hands on any type of evidence that they had on file. Also, who was the man at the Bingo Haven that would risk his career? What about the card in my purse? There were too many questions and no answers as of right now.

"Are you coming?" Officer James said as he popped his head back into the room.

"Oh, yes," I chuckled.

I got up from the table and followed both of the Officers back down the hall to the bullpen. Upon glancing around again, I saw several others working at their desks, who must have been following up on their own cases. *Why would Greenfield have so many cases that needed to be pursued? It's not like we were a very large town?*

"I see the puzzled look; many of our other Officers are on loan to other departments and consulting on other cases," Officer James filled me in.

I heard footsteps behind me, and I knew that it was Jasper from the other side of the interrogation area. He was able to quickly catch up, and I knew he had heard what Officer James had just said.

"Since I am now a Police consultant, what is the next step in the case?" I asked, my curiosity piqued as we had just come around to the pegboard with my picture pent upon it.

"First and foremost, we are going to take your picture down and put up one of just a question mark since we don't know who the murderer is," Officer Franks said.

I was relieved knowing that he had changed his mind, even if he didn't show it outwardly.

"I think on the TV shows, this is when you guys start to delve into the Bingo Haven's finances to see if there was any type of financial motive?" Jasper questioned.

"You watch a lot of crime shows?" Officer James asked.

"I am guilty of that," I laughed.

"Only a few every now and then," Jasper said.

"Uh huh," Officer James said.

After looking around the area where the peg board was, I saw both of their office cubicles where they had their personal belongings and pictures of their families. I tried to take in everything I could about what adorned their personal spaces. On Officer James' desk, there were pictures of who I presumed was his family. His wife with their two boys and their lovely home in the background. There were drawings from the children that littered every aspect of free space that had been available. There were also pictures of the boys with a fully grown german shepherd.

"Were you in the K9 unit? I questioned, unable to keep my curiosity at bay.

"I was," Officer James said. "Ronnie was up for retirement and was starting to show his age a little. The department made an executive decision, and I was awarded custody of the retired Officer. As long as I kept good care of him,"

"If your children are anything like you as a child, I'm sure he stays pretty fit," I laughed.

"My children are every bit of their father's son's,"

I looked over to Officer Franks office space, and it was also covered with pictures of his family but nothing of an immediate family. I saw pictures of his sisters with him on vacation and then with his parents.

"Before you scrutinize me, I just haven't found the right woman yet," he chimed in.

"No scrutiny, I haven't found the right person either," I laughed.

"Let's get back to the case," Jasper chimed in.

"Yes, you said that you have a forensic accountant going through the financial records?" I questioned, bringing the appropriate topic back at hand.

"Yes," Officer Franks said.

"Is there anything that we can do today?" I questioned.

"There are a few reports that we're waiting on from the lab and some other departments, so we just need to wait," Officer James said.

"In that case, I'm ready to head back home for the evening. It has been a long and trying day. Jasper?"

"I agree. Let me drop you back off at your house, and maybe we'll pick this up first thing in the morning?"

"Agreed,"

Jasper and I walked out of the Police Station and walked back to his now cold truck. It was nighttime, and I didn't realize how much time had passed, and my stomach grumbled.

"Before I take you home, you need to get something to eat. Let's go grab a bite at one of the smaller restaurants in town?"

With my stomach still grumbling, I didn't really have a choice but to agree with him.

"Fine, we'll go grab a bite to eat. Then will you take me home?"

"Of course, my friend!"

Jasper revved the engine to life and pulled out of the parking lot and down onto one of the side streets that would take me to my favorite pizza place.

"How did you know that I wanted pizza?" I laughed.

"Just had a hunch," he laughed back.

I loved the fall weather; it was crisp in the morning, warm in the afternoon, and then crisp again in the evening. I'm glad that I still had my jacket, or I would have been in big trouble. Jasper pulled into a parking space, and we both got out of the truck and headed inside the small eatery.

When we walked through the door, the bell chimed overhead to alert the workers that a customer had entered the building.

"Hello, Lola and Jasper! Nice to see you guys!" the owner of the shop shouted from behind the counter.

We proceeded to sit at an empty table away from the others who were already eating and began to look at the well-known menus. One of the younger female servers arrived at our table, and she smiled at both of us.

"The usual guys?" she smiled.

"Yes, please," Jasper and I said in unison.

We both broke out into laughter, and then the server grabbed our drinks and put our order into the computer system.

"On a more serious note," Jasper paused.

"What do we know about the case?" I finished his sentence for him.

"I'm guessing not much,"

"You would be right, but let's talk about something else. I'm tired of talking about the case for tonight,"

"I can't help it. The entire day has been playing on repeat inside of my mind, and it's the only thing I can think about,"

The young server came back with our drinks and our salads for the appetizer.

"Thank you," I said to her.

"The rest of the food will be out shortly," she smiled back.

Jasper slowly picked at his salad, but I devoured mine like I hadn't eaten in a long time. I had finished just in time when our small pizzas arrived.

"These just came out of the oven, so please be very careful," the owner said. "By the way, I don't believe the rumors that are going around town," he winked at me.

Even an older woman could be embarrassed. Who else in town already knew about the rumors of me being the suspect? I couldn't say anything; I just nodded at him in recognition and then began to devour my pizza.

"No leftovers?" Jasper asked.

"Not tonight," I said in between bites. "To be honest, I'm thinking about dessert,"

"You? That's something new," Jasper laughed.

"I can't help it," I'm a stress eater," I chided as I began to flip through the dessert menu.

I waved the server over, and when she had a free moment, she quickly came to our table.

"Is everything alright?" she asked.

"Everything was lovely. I would like to place a to-go dessert order, please," I said as I pointed to an entire chocolate cake.

"Just a slice or the entire cake?"

"The whole thing,"

"Of course, let me adjust your bill, and I'll be right back with that to-go order,"

I waited patiently while my friend finished his meal and then packaged his small amount of leftovers for another day. The server came back with my new bill, and the cake was already in a bag, ready for carrying. I left her a tip and paid my bill, then walked back out into the crisp air. I would have almost walked home, but I was afraid that I might freeze being out in the cool for too long. I don't keep the warmth like I used to back in my younger years.

"Ready?" Jasper asked as he rubbed his full stomach.

"Yes, I'm ready to go home,"

We got back into the truck, and with the engine still partially warm, the heat kicked on immediately once it was started. I stared blankly out the window, and it seemed like minutes had ticked by, and we were suddenly at my home.

I heard a faint voice that seemed to be trying to get my attention.

"Lola?" Jasper's voice rang through me.

"Huh? Where are we?"

"Your house,"

"Oh, so soon?"

"Do you need me to walk you to your door?"

"No, I think that I'll be alright. Thank you for always being my friend and being there for me," I said with slight tears in my eyes.

I got out of the truck, walked to my door, unlocked it, and walked inside. My cat didn't greet me as soon as I walked in, so she must have already been asleep. Today has been rather unusual because she wasn't used to me being out late at night, not even when there were tournaments at the Bingo Halls. I didn't bother turning on any lights because I knew my way around. I walked into the kitchen and put my cake in the microwave so it would be safe.

The answering machine that I still had in place had the number three flashing in the darkness. Somebody must have left a few messages while I was out today. I decided not to listen to the messages tonight because my mind was becoming a garbled mess.

I heard a faint meow sound coming from my room, and it brought a smile to my face. Deep inside, I was glad to start the evening process of getting ready for bed. I went to the bathroom to wash my face before changing into my night clothes. When I flicked on the bedroom light, my beautiful cat sat there waiting for me to come to bed.

"Alright, I'm coming," I said softly.

When I lay in bed, she snuggled up next to me and purred, lulling me to sleep.

Although falling asleep was rather easy, staying asleep was another issue. I woke up almost every hour on the hour. The last time I rolled over and looked at the clock, it read four in the morning. The loud purring sounds called me back to sleep, and when I closed my eyes one final time, deep sleep finally took over.

FOUR

I rolled over and no longer felt the purring machine that had slept next to me all night. My eyes fluttered open because something didn't feel right; my cat was always with me whenever I slept. We usually awoke around six in the morning, but after quickly putting on my glasses, I was able to read the clock on my nightstand, which read ten. I blinked hard a couple of times, not sure if what I was reading was right, and bolted out of bed.

The sound of my phone ringing disturbed my thoughts, and I quickly changed course from the kitchen to the living room.

"Hello?" I answered.

Nobody replied back, but I could hear their breathy sounds coming from the other end of the call.

"Hello?" I said again.

Nobody answered.

"If somebody doesn't answer me, I'm going to hang up!" I said a little hysterically.

Suddenly, I heard the line click as though they hung up, and I did the same. Startled, I set my phone back on the receiver and saw that there were five messages on the machine. I still wasn't in the right mindset and walked away from the recording device.

"Jinx," I called out as I began to look for my siamese cat.

I waited momentarily, listening for any sounds of life. Nothing.

"Jinx, where are you?" I called out again.

I walked around the house looking for her when suddenly, a severe draft in the house caught my attention. I walked over to my kitchen and saw a brick lying on the floor as though somebody was trying to send a message. There was broken glass everywhere, and I had to be careful where I stepped. The hole in the window was large enough for my cat to escape, and my heart sank knowing that I might not ever find her again.

The telephone ringing caught my attention again. Who could it be now?

"Hello?" I answered.

"Hey, Lola! It's Jasper. I'm outside in the neighborhood, and I thought I just saw Jinx taking a stroll on the sidewalk?" he asked, a little confused.

"Oh, Jasper! It is her! Can you catch her and bring her back here?"

"Yeah, but how did she get out?"

"When you come over, you can see for yourself,"

"I'll see what I can do, then I'll be right over,"

The call was quickly disconnected, and I walked back to my room to get ready for the day. No point in the Police seeing me in my pajamas. I quickly readied myself, including shoes that were sustainable for cleaning up a glass mess. I walked back toward the phone and began to call Officer James' desk to report the crime.

"This is Officer James," his voice sounded over the phone.

"Hello, this is Lola. I need to report a crime,"

"Miss Lola, is everything alright?"

"It seems somebody has vandalized my home by throwing a brick through my kitchen window. There is glass and debris chunks everywhere. My cat Jinx even escaped,"

"I'll be right over. Don't clean up anything. We need to take pictures for evidence,"

"See you soon,"

I hung up the call, went away from the mess in the kitchen, and sat in my cream-colored chair to drown out my own thoughts. Who would want to hurt me?

A knock on the door drew me from my thoughts, and when I peeked out of the living room windows, I saw Jasper's truck parked in the driveway. I got up and hurried to the door to let him in.

"I found her!" he exclaimed excitedly. "How did she get out?"

"By the gaping hole in my kitchen window from where somebody started to remodel my home without my permission," I said sadly as I took my cat from his arms.

She jumped to me with happiness as though she never wanted to be outside again.

"What?" Jasper asked, shocked.

"Go take a look for yourself. Just don't touch any of the evidence; Officer James is on his way over now to process the scene."

Jasper left me and made his way to the kitchen. I went back to my chair, cat still in hand, and sat down at my chair once more. I began to stroke her absent-mindedly, and she purred from the touch.

"Who on Earth could have done this?" Jasper's raised voice bellowed through the house.

"That's a good question," I mumbled.

After Jasper was finished with his preliminary examination of the rest of my home, he went to sit across from me in his usual spot on the couch. Usually, Jinx would have run to him, but for once, she stayed put and continued to purr loudly for everyone to hear.

About an hour had passed before one Police cruiser pulled onto the street in front of my house.

"What took them so long?" Jasper muttered.

I laughed slightly because it was unusual for his patience to wear so thin so early in the day.

"I mean, literally, it's almost one in the afternoon," he continued.

"Hush, they probably were called to do some other important work," I countered.

"Yeah, go on a lunch run or chase after some donuts,"

I laughed, but they did take an awfully long time to get here. Before I could get up, Jasper launched himself and took off toward the door.

"Hello, Jasper," Officer James greeted.

"What took so long?" Jasper asked.

"Lunch," Office Franks said.

"I see; you still have some of it on your uniform. Was it subs with extra sauce?" Jasper fired back.

"Sorry about that; we were up pretty early waiting on the reports to come back from the other case," Officer James said.

All three men were now in my small living room, but I gestured for them to take a seat if they so desired. Officer James did, but not Officer Franks. Jasper continued to stand as though he was a bouncer waiting to throw these two outside at any moment.

"Any news?" I questioned.

"Not that we can openly discuss," Officer Franks said with a little disappointment.

I pursed my lips but didn't say anything else on the matter.

"Jasper, would you please show these two where the damage to my house has been done. I did as you said and didn't touch anything so you could catalog and document everything," I asked.

All three men left the living room, and I felt a heavy presence leave with them. Jinx yawned but continued to stay on my lap.

"My goodness, that's a large brick and an even larger hole in the window," Officer Franks gawked.

"Did you hear anything last night?" Officer James shouted.

"No, I was tossing and turning all night, but around four in the morning, I finally fell into a deep sleep. I'm not even sure what time Jinx had gotten out this morning," I replied.

"I found her not far from your house, so she couldn't have been out for too long," Jasper said.

I continued to pet Jinx as the men talked back and forth. I couldn't keep up with their rapid-fire questioning, so I began to drown out their voices. I hummed softly to myself, and I leaned back in the chair and closed my eyes. The events from yesterday began to play out in my mind, but I didn't want them to. The victim giving me a note stating not to trust anybody, then finding him dead just moments later. *What did he know that would have cost him his life?* I hummed a little louder to keep the distraction of voices from my thoughts. *Was he investigating something?* The song I had hummed was over, but I continued to hum it over and over again while my thoughts raced back and forth.

"Did you say something?" Jasper said as he walked back into the living room.

"Huh?" I said as I was brought back from my thoughts.

"You were talking about something?" Jasper replied.

"I was?" I asked, confused.

"You were uttering something about the case, I'm guessing. Something about him investigating something?" Jasper paused.

"Oh, I didn't realize that I had said anything out loud. I was just pondering on the thought of the victim being some type of personal investigator?"

Both of the Officers came in with frowns on their faces as though I said something.

"What is it?" Jasper asked.

"Miss. Lola is right. Mr. Burchfield liked to play detective sometimes; when something went wrong in the area, he liked to try to play hero," Officer Franks said quietly.

"How did you figure that out?" Officer James asked with a grin.

For the first time in a few hours, I got up from the chair and went over to get my purse from a cabinet that I had always kept it in. I pulled out the bingo card with the written note on it and began to walk back to the living room.

"Here," I said as I handed over the note.

"What is this?" Officer James asked.

"Thomas left that on the table when he had gotten up from his seat,"

Both Officers had read the note but had puzzled looks on their faces.

"You didn't think that this was important information for us to have known?" Officer Franks said, clearly frustrated.

"I haven't even listened to my voice messages from yesterday. So, with everything that has been going on, I honestly forgot about it," I said.

Officer Franks just waved his hand in the air and walked outside as though he was trying not to say something that he would later regret.

"We'll need to take this into evidence. We are done with our report on the window, too. I'll call a buddy of mine and have him come put a piece of plywood over it so Jinx doesn't get out again, and a slight piece of mind. That is if it's ok with you?" Officer James asked.

"That would be lovely," I replied.

Officer James nodded his head in agreement and then walked outside with his partner. I went back to my chair and sat down briefly to watch both Officers. Officer Franks got in the cruiser, and Officer James immediately pulled out his cell and made a quick call to whom I would have guessed to be his friend.

"I better go get that mess cleaned up before Jinx hurts one of her paws," I said sadly.

"Would you like some company?" Jasper asked.

"Right now, I would rather be alone if that's okay."

"Alright, I'll call you later tonight to check on you,"

"Thank you,"

"Oh, and Lola. Please eat something, you haven't eaten since you woke up,"

As though Jasper could read my thoughts, my stomach growled in protest.

"Thank you for the kind words, Jasper, but I need to get this mess cleaned up first. Then I'll make Jinx and me something small to eat,"

"I'll see myself out," Jasper replied with a small frown.

I watched him from the windows walk with his head down and his hands in his pockets until he reached his truck. I took my attention off of him briefly to ensure Jinx wasn't going to hurt herself or try to escape again. I watched her climb on my mountainous bookshelves, and one fell out and onto the floor.

"Jinx, how did you do that?" I asked out loud.

She meowed back as though to say she was sorry, but it was fascinating that the book that she dropped happened to be a mystery book that I had read many years ago. I was about to put it back in its place when a picture had fallen out of it. It fell gracefully to the floor, and when I bent over to pick it up, I recognized it to be one when the Bingo Haven had first opened. Jasper and I were standing with a man whom I hardly recognized but remembered him as being one of the business associates who dealt with Ruby and the actual owner.

Jinx's mewing brought me back to the present, and I quickly went to the kitchen to begin the rigorous cleaning that was going to need to be done. I needed to ensure all of the glass would get picked up or risk cutting my feet in the middle of the night.

As I walked into the kitchen, I looked around, and there was glass everywhere. When I saw the chocolate cake from last night, my stomach growled so loud that it actually hurt.

"A quick piece of cake wouldn't hurt," I said to Jinx.

She mewed back at me and began to purr as though that was her thought exactly. With her permission, I walked over to the cupboard, grabbed a small plate, and then went over to where I kept the silverware. I pulled out a knife and a fork so I could divvy out a small piece. Before I went to the table, I grabbed a glass and poured some cold milk into it. With a cup and plate in hand, I walked over to the table and sat down to enjoy the small piece of sugary goodness.

Once finished, I set my plate and cup to the side; since my sink was full of glass, I couldn't wash my dishes. When I walked back toward the sink, the shadow of somebody standing there caught me off guard.

"Who are you?" I shouted at the man.

"Oliver called me, ma'am. To come and cover up the hole in the window?" he replied.

"Your Officer James' friend?" I questioned.

"Yes, ma'am. From what I was able to see, we are going to need to finish breaking the glass so that way when whoever fixes it won't make a bigger mess," the man said.

"Good thing I haven't cleaned it up yet,"

"I'm Alan. You know, if you wanted, I could give you a quote to fix it and maybe be back out in a couple of days if you would like?"

"That would be fine,"

"Alright, stand back. I'm going to finish breaking the glass,"

I did as he asked, grabbed Jinx from the counter, and walked her into the living room.

"You be good, and don't try to escape," I chided her.

I walked back into the kitchen area to the sounds of more glass breaking into my home. *It really was a good thing that I hadn't cleaned.*

"I can help you clean all that up if you would like?" Alan asked.

"No, it will be ok. I need something to do anyway, to take my mind off of things,"

"Have you heard the rumors that are going around town saying that one of the local residents murdered a man down at the Bingo Haven?" Alan asked wide-eyed.

"Oh, I've heard," I replied.

"I don't think somebody could have done it, I mean, it was a Bingo Hall. What really goes on at a bingo place where the older generations like to hang out?" Alan half spoke to himself as he was taking measurements of the window.

"I go to the Bingo Haven,"

"Well, I mean..." he paused.

"I'm only teasing you. I know that I'm elderly, and that is where the good gossip comes from," I said while getting the broom and my vacuum.

I left him momentarily to go and get my cleaning tools when the sounds of ringing were coming from my phone again. I quickly changed course and quickened my pace to the telephone.

"Hello?" I answered.

There was nobody on the other end. The same heavy breathing as earlier today.

I didn't have the patience for this, so I hung up the call and went back to my closet for the tools so I could finally clean up the mess.

"I'm done with breaking all of the glass. I'm going to grab the plywood and start to put it against the bigger hole that I put into the wall," he said with a smile.

As he went to get the material, I began to vacuum the small pieces of glass into the bagless container. I watched as the small crystals were reflecting off of the light.

Before I was finished with the vacuum, he was back with the large piece of plywood, and he began to set it in place, causing the kitchen to darken.

"Well, I certainly didn't expect that," I said to myself.

I heard the sounds of a drill, and I knew that he was using screws to set it in place so nothing would knock it down.

I made quick work from the windowsill and the counters, ensuring that I had gotten every small piece. Once finished, I quickly went to work on the floor. I grabbed the broom for the bigger pieces and then used the sweeper again for the small nooks and crannies.

I heard a small knocking sound coming from the front door. I set down my tools once again and went to greet whom I assumed would be Alan.

"I'm all done for now, but here is the estimate for me to replace the window and any of the trimming, too," he said as he handed over the paper with a smile.

"Thank you, Alan, I'll be giving you a call in a few days, I suppose,"

"You haven't even looked at the price yet,"

"It's damage done to my home, and I'm going to need to have it fixed sooner or later. Why don't you go ahead and order any material that you would need and call me once it comes in?"

"Yes, ma'am," he nodded, showing his appreciation, and walked back to his truck.

I closed the door and went back to the kitchen again to hopefully finish cleaning the mess on the floor once and for all.

FIVE

A few hours passed, and I continuously checked every crevice in my kitchen to ensure that I had picked up all of the pieces. I was finally satisfied with my work and began to put away my cleaning tools. When I went back to the kitchen, I was about to look out the window over my sink, but I suddenly remembered the plywood over the hole. It dampened my mood, so I left the kitchen entirely and went back to my chair. The day had quickly gone from bright and shiny to dark and gloomy. The wind picked up, and I knew it was going to storm any minute.

No sooner than I blinked, I saw lightning flash and heard thunder roaring across the area. It startled Jinx, who quickly jumped into my lap, and I began to stroke her fur to help calm her. After a few moments of calming motions, she started to purr slightly. I picked up the crossword puzzle from yesterday, but I couldn't keep my concentration. I set it back down on the stand beside me. I contemplated what I wanted out of the day, but nothing came to mind. I shook my head to bring my thoughts back to the present day, and while picking up Jinx, I carried her to the kitchen so I could start a pot of coffee.

I gently set her down and washed my hands before I pulled the fresh coffee grounds out of a cabinet, opened the container, and began to divvy out the portion sizes I would need. I was getting the water ready to put into the chamber at the back of the machine when another flash of lightning lit up my dimly lit house. Within seconds, the thunder bellowed across the area once again.

"Jinx, I think this storm is here to stay for a while. We might as well get comfy,"

My beautiful siamese mewed at me as though she could have read my mind. I quickly turned back to my coffee pot and turned it on, and then went back to the living room so I could watch the storm from my chair.

Usually, I would hear Jinx's bell from her collar as she followed me around the house, but this time, she was nowhere near me. This made me pause momentarily, but after considering all the options, I assumed she went back to the bedroom to hide from the storm.

As I walked back into the living room, I saw something sticking out of the couch on which Officer James was sitting earlier.

"Strange?"

I didn't notice this earlier?

I quickly went over to the couch, pulled the file folder out of its hiding place, and contemplated on whether I should open it or not.

"After all, Jinx, he did leave it here..." I said out loud.

Not waiting another moment, I carefully opened the file, and there were dozens of papers neatly tucked inside of it. It was the forensic files from the Bingo Haven. I got up from the couch and went back over to my chair to better see in the light. I had just begun to scour through a couple of pieces from the numerous documents when another thunderous sound shattered my concentration. It was so loud that it almost shook the house. The sudden beeping noises from the coffee pot finishing up brought me to the sweet aroma that had filled my home.

Coffee.

There was only the thought of getting a nice hot cup into my frazzled system to hopefully calm me down. *Coffee to calm one's nerves?*

I walked back into the kitchen, made myself a delicious cup, and then headed back into the living room. The rain continued to pound onto the pavement, and the wind howled from the outside, causing the last bit of leaves to fall from the trees.

"Winter will be here before you know it. I hope Alan gets those parts ordered soon. I don't want to lose any heat from the disaster," I said into the empty house.

I half expected to hear Jinx's mews, but there was nothing but the void of an old house. I settled back into my cozy chair and looked at the clock; it read five at night. I must have dozed off in my chair watching the storm, which was now down to a light drizzle.

"Jinx?" I called out.

Her purring from a spot on the couch caught my attention, and it brought a smile to my face.

"Jinx, it's dinner time, and I haven't laid a thing out to cook. Looks like it's take-out," I smiled.

I got up, stretched, then walked over to the desk and pulled out a handful of menus until I found one that I liked.

"How does Chinese food sound?" I called out as I began to dial the buttons on the home phone.

I glanced back down at the phone's base, and it still had the number five flashing on it. I just remembered the messages! I quickly ordered an enormous amount of food so I could have leftovers, went over to the desk, and grabbed a pen and paper so I could take down the messages.

"Message One. Hello, this is Cindy from the Dentist's office calling to confirm your scheduled appointment. Please give us a call back to confirm or cancel the appointment. Thank you!" the phone base said.

I quickly jotted down the information so I could confirm the appointment when I had a free moment.

"Message Two. Hello, this message is for Lola; this is Brian calling from the Greenfield County Hospital about some billing issues with your insurance. Please give me a call back to straighten this out," the phone base said.

I again jotted down the information to take care of this later.

"Message Three. Hello, Lola. You don't know me, but I know you. I've been watching you at the Bingo Haven for quite some time. I find it kind of funny that you and Jasper think that you can outwit me," a deep male voice said before cutting off.

I sat back, stunned for a moment. *Who was this person calling me? Was it the murderer? Do they know where I live?*

Message Four. Nothing but heavy breathing.

Message Five. Nothing but heavy breathing.

I brought myself out of my stupor of questions and quickly saved the messages so I could go back and listen to them again. There was a sudden knock on the door, and when I looked through the peephole, it was the delivery person with my food.

"Just a moment!" I shouted.

"I've got an order for a Lola?" a male teenage voice shouted.

I rushed over to my purse, grabbed the cash needed for the food, and made my way to the front door. After we exchanged money for food, I gave him a tip, then closed the door and deadbolted it behind me. With food in hand, I went to the back door and ensured that it was locked. I set the food down and began to lock all of the windows. A wave of paranoia set in, but I brushed it off and went back to the food in the kitchen. I set out the food that I wanted for tonight and portioned out the sizes that I thought I would be able to eat. I put the rest in the fridge and grabbed a can of soda in return, then headed for the kitchen table.

I ate in silence, and Jinx ate her cat food when I saw the folder sitting on the table. I must have set it down earlier when I went to get a cup of coffee. I opened it again, and the dozens of pages stayed in place since they were on a flat surface. I read each piece very carefully, digesting the information. There were several bits starting to not add up. I checked the revenue from the players and all of the incoming money, but there was more going out of the business than it was making. *Where was the extra money coming from?*

I went over the same information a few more times to make sure that I understood everything. There was definitely more money going out of the business than coming in. *How was the business staying afloat?* I looked at the ledgers, and there were several checks that were coming in multiple times a month, and it looked to be all from the same person. I'd have to check in with Officer James tomorrow. I would also have to admit that I went over the file that he had left for me.

With a guilty conscience, I closed the file and went to clean the few dishes that I had used before going back to my chair to check on the storm again. Jinx's bell towed behind me, and it brought a huge smile to my face. I peered out the windows, and it had completely died down; the wind was no longer threatening to tear everything down in its path.

I squinted my eyes, and that was when I saw the huge tree that had been blown into the road. There was a sudden flickering from the lights, then I was in total darkness.

"Great. A power outage," I said out loud.

I left my living room and headed down the hallway, feeling my way around the house. I knew I had a flashlight in my room just in case I ever woke up to the lights being out. I felt around until I reached the dresser, then felt around some more for what I needed.

"Found you," I said, wrapping my hand around the handle.

I flicked it on, and a small amount of illumination came from it. I need to remember to change the batteries soon, or the next time I need this, I might not have anything.

With a small amount of light, I headed back to the living room to try to see anything, but it was already dark out. The only thing that I was able to see clearly was the lights coming from the fire department vehicles from down the road.

That was fast.

There were also several crew members who looked to be from the electric company since they had their logo on their safety jackets, and they started immediately getting to work.

This is the first time they have been in such a hurry. I wonder what happened? Too bad I can't turn on the news to find out.

There was nothing else for me to do, so I turned off the flashlight, sat in the darkness, and allowed the artificial lights from the outside beam into my house. After all, the Firefighters can't move the tree in the dark.

I assumed that a little over an hour had passed, which would have made it almost slightly after six, when I saw Jasper's red truck pull into my driveway. *What was he thinking?*

I went to the door, unlocked the deadbolt, and waited for him to rush through the rain, which had started to pick up again.

"What are you doing here?" I asked sternly.

"You know how worried I get," he started.

"You are such a worry wart. I swear," I said, laughing, as I let him inside.

"I tried to call you on your cell, but it went straight to voicemail," he began.

"It must have died,"

"You? Let your phone die?"

"I have been busy today, Jasper. Did you come over because you needed something, or were you genuinely worried?"

"I was worried..."

I waited to see if he was going to say anything else, but he didn't.

"I have something I want to show you," I said, heading to the kitchen.

He stayed silent and followed me throughout my house. I went into the kitchen first and pulled the file forward onto the table.

"You're going to want to sit down for this," I began.

I went and grabbed the flashlight from the living room and

quickly headed back. Jasper already had the flashlight from his phone and was going through the papers like a madman.

"You know math was not my favorite subject," he laughed.

"Do you know what you're looking at?" I asked.

He pondered momentarily but then shook his head no.

"It's the forensic documents from the Bingo Haven,"

Jasper's eyes got so wide that I thought they would pop out.

"You mean these documents from the Police Station about the case? How did you get them?"

"I found them in between the couch cushions. Officer James must have left them there on purpose, knowing that I would find them. The question is, why did he leave it, and what does he want us to do about it?" I asked.

Jasper sat back in the chair, which he had claimed for the time being, and I could tell that this really bothered him. He had been my best friend for several years. Although we did give the romantic side a try, it just wasn't meant to be. We knew that both of us were better off being friends.

The light flickered back on, and Jasper checked the time on his phone.

"It's just a little after nine,"

"Are you serious? Where has the day gotten to?"

Jasper had gotten up from his seat and walked over toward me with a serious look. I couldn't place it, but there must have been something that he wasn't telling me.

"Lola, is there anything that you're not telling me?" he asked.

"Funny, I was about to ask you the same thing,"

He briefly looked at his phone but shook his head instead.

"I'll see myself out. I'll be by sometime in the morning unless you need me sooner. Just give me a call." he left abruptly and didn't say another word.

I followed after him and ensured the deadbolt was back in place before heading toward the hallway that led to my room. I didn't have any reason to stay up and ponder about why Jasper had been acting so weird. I wanted the thoughts to just leave me alone, but they continued to plague me no matter where in the house I went to. I went to the bedroom, lay down, and waited for Jinx to jump onto the bed in her assigned spot before closing my eyes and allowing myself to drift away.

SIX

I awoke startled due to the fact that somebody had been pounding on my front door. I quickly put on a robe and put on my house slippers to investigate who the culprit was. *Probably, the paperboy who liked to throw mine on top of my roof probably out of spite.*

As I got to the door, the pounding became more erratic, and it was starting to scare me a little.

"Who is it?" I called from behind the massive locked door.

"Lola, open up," Jasper's voice called out.

What on Earth does he think he's doing? Pounding on my door in the middle of the night, or is it early morning?

I unlocked the door and there stood my disheveled friend. He didn't look like himself, very unkept. His clothes weren't their usual tidy self, and it looked as though he didn't shave this morning.

"What's wrong?" I asked, still standing in the doorway.

He rushed inside and began to look throughout the house as though he was on a mission. I shut the door behind him and locked it again. The thought of the creepy message jolted into my mind, causing me to wake up just a bit more. I paid him no heed to whatever it was that he had decided was most important this morning and began to walk into the kitchen. I slowly but surely made enough coffee for the both of us.

I sat down at the kitchen table and yawned while he continued his investigation.

"What are you looking for?" I asked sleepily.

"Shh..."

"Well, good morning to you, too?" I mumbled.

After another thirty minutes of him searching and looking defeated, he came and sat at the table.

"I was looking for listening devices," he admitted.

I didn't say anything because my usually well-dressed friend looked ragged, as though he didn't sleep well last night.

"Did you get any sleep?" I asked.

"What?"

"You pound on my door at seven in the morning to come in and look for listening devices?"

"Ok, when you put it that way, it sounds a bit ridiculous," he blushed.

"Where did you get the idea in your head that there would be listening devices in my home?"

"I'd rather not say..."

I didn't want to argue with Jasper, but he was acting weirder than usual, and it was starting to get on my nerves.

"You can't just barge in here for no good reason and act like a madman," I said a little louder than needed.

He didn't respond but looked at his phone as though he was contemplating if he should be telling me something. I got up from the table and went over to the coffee pot because I was getting so frustrated with him. He had officially overstepped his boundaries.

"Alright, I guess I should confess before you throw me out of your house," he paused while I continued to make a cup of coffee. "When I got home last night, there was a package on the front porch. I thought it was odd that the delivery service would be out so late, especially with the power being out. I picked it up, took it to the house, and gently set it on the counter. It wasn't addressed to anybody, and I thought it was a box that had blown into my yard and got caught by the front door,"

I walked away from the coffee pot and sat back down beside him, waiting for him to continue. I began to blow lightly on my coffee to cool it down so as not to burn my mouth.

"When I opened the box to break it down for the garbage, there was something inside of it. It had a note typed out neatly, saying *She is never alone.* I set aside the paper and pulled out a receiver that could only listen, and it was your voice coming from the device,"

I stopped drinking my coffee when he paused again.

"I didn't stop anywhere last night, and since we don't live that far apart, it didn't take me long to get home. I heard you talking to Jinx about going to bed. I'm one hundred percent positive that it was your voice coming from the receiver. I was so freaked out that I dropped the receiver and broke part of it. There was something else,"

I took another sip of coffee to try and steady my nerves.

"There was a symbol on the back of the paper that I know was intentionally left for me. It's something that was super simple, but it's from my past,"

"What was the symbol?"

"Three dots in the shape of a triangle,"

"How do you know that it's from your past?"

"Call it a gut feeling,"

I sat back in my chair and contemplated what Jasper had told me. If he was able to hear me talking in my empty home, where would the listening device be?

"I think we need to bring in Officer James and have him sweep my house immediately. Do you still have the receiver?" I asked.

"I put it in the truck,"

"Let me go get dressed, and you make yourself a giant cup of coffee for the road. You sure look like you need it,"

I drank the last of my drink, headed to the bedroom, and shut the door as tight as possible. I quickly readied myself for the day and then went back out to join Jasper.

"Do you want to head to the station?" he asked.

"Yes, let me grab my purse,"

As I walked into the living room, the lights flashing on my answering machine reminded me that I hadn't told Jasper about the voicemail left on my phone.

"Ready?" he asked with a giant thermos full of coffee.

"Actually, before we head out, there is something that I need to tell you. Sometime while we were out, I received a message,"

I began to play the messages, bypassed the first two, and let him listen to the third. I watched as his eyes widened, and shock was written on his posture.

"We need to go," he said as I saved the message again.

"One more thing! I need to grab the file from yesterday," I said as I went back to the kitchen.

I headed back to the door, locked it from the outside, and then made my way toward Jasper's truck.

"Happy?" he asked.

"I have a few questions that I wanted to ask him. You know, since we are already heading to the Station?"

"I guess that makes sense," he said, shrugging.

He started the engine, and the heat, which he had forgotten to turn off, blasted me in the face.

"Were you cold?" I laughed, shutting the vents.

"Yes, as a matter of fact, I was," he laughed.

Neither of us said anything else the entire way to the Station. It was still early morning, and I wasn't sure if Officer James had made it in yet. Or at least maybe he was in, but Officer Franks wasn't. That man really needed to work on his people skills.

I had been staring out the window with no particular thought in mind, but now that we had made it to the Station, I noticed a few things that seemed to darken my mood.

"What's wrong?"

"What if Officer James didn't mean to leave the file?" I asked.

"What do you mean?"

"What if he had it but had forgotten it when we called to report the damage to my house?" I questioned.

"You have a point. Let's not mention the file to him until we know for sure that he left it for you. Let's just see if they have any new developments and report what happened,"

I didn't respond, only nodded my head in agreement. I got out of the truck, headed inside, and looked around to see if Officer James had arrived. As I was looking around for him, I bumped into somebody.

"Excuse me," I said, startled.

"That's ok, I wasn't looking where I was going," Officer James said.

"Just the person I was looking for. Is Officer Franks in yet?" I asked.

"No, something came up, and he won't be able to make it in today. Why do you ask?"

"No reason in particular. He just needs to work on his people skills," I laughed.

"No kidding. I keep telling him that, but does he listen," Officer James laughed as he directed us through the bullpen.

Not much more was added to the board since a few days ago. I frowned, hoping they were a little farther along than what they seemed to have gathered.

"Is this all that you have?" I questioned.

Jasper came in right behind us with his thermos in hand. I glanced in his direction to see what he thought about the board, but he didn't seem to pay too much attention.

I guess since he wasn't going to be much help, then I needed to take a closer look.

"May I?" I asked.

"Sure, you are, after all, no longer a suspect,"

I nodded my thanks and began to inspect the board closer. There were a few statements from the crowd, but not much. There was a forensic file with a piece of fabric that they discovered near the body.

"Officer James? Where was this piece of fabric found? I mean, where exactly was it discovered?" I questioned.

"The forensics team discovered it underneath the victim, as though he grabbed ahold of somebody as he was killed. I thought it was odd seeing that it was so small..." Officer James's voice trailed off.

"How much time was there from when the body was killed to being discovered?" Jasper asked.

Excellent question.

"According to the M.E. report no more than 5 minutes," Officer James said.

"Since we were both there, I would say that is about accurate," I added.

"Did you take a look at the forensic file I dropped off?" Officer James asked.

"I didn't want to mention it in case you had accidentally left it behind," I added.

"I did leave it behind so you could tell me your thoughts about what you think is going on?" Officer James said.

"Hate to change the subject, but there was another reason we also needed to stop by today. I'm not sure, but I think we need to either add something to the case or file a report of some kind," Jasper said.

Officer James leaned back in his chair and looked both of us over.

"Tell me what happened," he said.

I began with the voicemail that was left at my home. Jasper proceeded to explain about the receiver and how my house was bugged with listening devices.

"This is serious. How would somebody be able to get into your home and place devices?" Officer James.

"I'm not sure. I haven't been able to work through that," I admitted.

Jasper began to skim through the information that was on the board.

"Anything out of place?" I questioned.

"There are a few things out of place from the Bingo Haven. Since I work there part-time, I know the inside of that building almost like the back of my hand," Jasper said.

"Why don't you guys go back to the scene of the crime and take another look around and see if we missed anything. I'm sure the forensics gathered all of the necessary fibers and stuff. Still, there might be something that we overlooked," Officer James said.

"That sounds like a plan. What about the receiver and the voicemail?" I asked.

"Did you bring the receiver with you?" Officer James inquired.

"Yes, it's in the truck. I can also grab the file if you would like?" Jasper asked.

"That would be great," I replied.

It took Jasper no time to head out to his truck and then back again.

"Here is the receiver, and here is the file," he said, a little breathless.

"Are you alright?" I questioned.

"Just need to do a little more cardio, that's all," he laughed.

He handed over both items, and Officer James put the receiver in an evidence bag. Then, he filled out a slight bit of paperwork before turning his attention back to us.

"So about that file?" Officer James asked.

"I found a few discrepancies," I admitted.

"We did, too. How would you explain it?" Officer James asked.

"Somebody is extorting money through the Bingo Haven," I gasped.

"Excellent. How do you prove it?" Officer James questioned.

"We need more evidence," Jasper chimed in.

"Yes, now do either of you have any other questions?"

"Not at this time. We will get back to you once we have further investigated the Bingo Haven," I replied.

"Talk with you soon," Officer James said.

Jasper and I left the Station and headed outside into the early winter morning.

"I didn't realize that winter was so close?" I said, laughing.

"I told you the weather forecast just last week!" Jasper griped.

"I didn't listen; you know I only take one day at a time," I said, rubbing my hands in the frigid morning weather.

"It will hopefully warm up soon,"

My phone began to ring in my purse. *Strange, I don't remember charging it last night.*

"Hello?" I answered.

"Hello, Lola? This is Alan," the voice said.

"Oh, Alan! Yes, were you able to get the parts to fix my window?"

"Yes, they came in earlier than expected. I have a few more things to pick up before I can repair the window fully. Could I come over tomorrow and begin the repairs?"

"Yes, that would be lovely. See you then."

"See you tomorrow,"

I hung up the phone and got inside Jasper's truck, and he began to side-eye me.

"Cat got your tongue?" I asked.

"Everything ok?" he asked sarcastically.

"Yes, everything is more than ok. Alan will be by tomorrow to fix my window,"

"That's great. Are you ready to head over to the Bingo Haven and see what we can find?"

"Yes,"

"You know that we might get banned for life?" he said, smiling.

"Exciting, isn't it?"

"As long as you know what we're getting into,"

"Jasper, I've always known what we're getting into. It's normally you who I have to convince otherwise,"

"Not this time, I guess," he said as he pulled out of the parking lot and headed into traffic.

SEVEN

I usually didn't like to be driven around like somebody important, but I could tell that Jasper was a little on edge, so I made an exception. We made it to the Bingo Haven about an hour before they opened. I looked at the outside of the building, and it still looked like the same old Bingo Haven, but there was something darker that would forever stain the history of this place now.

"Ready?" I asked as I unbuckled my seatbelt.

"As ready as I'll ever be,"

Both of us got out of the truck and headed inside. Nobody said a word to Jasper, but I could tell that I was getting a lot of side-eyed attention.

"Do you think that they will stop staring?" I asked.

"Eventually, once we capture the real killer," Jasper said.

I allowed Jasper to lead the way, and thankfully, it was away from the main parlor area where everybody was getting ready to start their shifts.

"Where are we going? I thought the main place to investigate would be the actual crime scene?" I asked.

"You would think that, but in fact, the real place we need to be looking is with the cleaning services," he replied, his tone carrying a hint of excitement.

"Why would we be looking for the cleaning services crew?"

"Think about it. Everything that happens around here, they would be the ones to get the most information. They hear the rumors and would get the most gossip," he said excitedly.

"I understand now! They would have been the ones who were cleaning up the leftover mess from the forensic team," I said, my voice reflecting a newfound confidence in our plan.

He headed down a set of stairs that led to the basement and we suddenly heard a set of female voices shouting at one another.

"What are you doing down here?" one voice said.

"I came here looking for the owner to discuss a business deal?" the second voice said.

"Sorry, he hasn't been around for a while. He left me in charge. Why did you find it necessary to speak down in the basement?" the first female asked.

I suddenly recognized who the voices were. The first one was Ruby, and the other was Victoria.

"I happened to see you down here," Victoria said.

"Nobody happens to walk down a flight of stairs and wander into the basement?" Ruby said skeptically.

"Fine, you caught me. I was meeting a secret lover of mine," Victoria laughed.

"Still not buying it. Why don't we make our way up to the actual office and discuss this business that you said you had," Ruby replied.

I peeked around the corner to try and get a look at the women, but I could only catch a glimpse.

Ruby was leaning against the washer and dryer, wearing a noncomplacent look. Then there was Victoria, who looked more nervous than ever.

I quickly stepped back so neither of them would notice me.

"After you," Victoria said.

"We have to move. Now!" I whispered to Jasper.

Both of us backed out of the stair hallway, rushed back to another level, and hid down a separate hall. I was able to hear the footfalls from both women because their boots made different clicking noises as they walked.

"I think we should follow them instead of looking for the cleaning crew," Jasper whispered from our hidden spot.

"I agree,"

After we were sure they were far enough away but not too far for us to follow, we left our hidden spot.

"Where do you think this is going?" I asked quietly.

"The office is on the top floor," Jasper said as he looked around to ensure nobody was watching as we followed the women.

"Have you been in the office before?" I chidded.

"Yes, there was a pay discrepancy on one of my paychecks, and Ruby wanted to talk with me personally,"

I shook my head but followed him throughout the maze of hallways that would eventually lead to the office.

"How are we going to listen to their conversation without getting caught?" I asked.

"I didn't think that far ahead," Jasper whispered.

As we continued to walk down the hallway, looking for any way to listen in, both of us discovered another office right beside it. Both of us turned and nodded at one another because we both knew this was going to be our best bet.

"Get to the point, Victoria," Ruby said.

"With that nasty murder that literally just happened, your business is going to plummet. Our businesses should merge and become one ultimate bingo hall," Victoria said.

There was a thud as though something was dropped on top of the desk.

"Is this your supposed business plan?" Ruby asked.

"Yes," Victoria replied.

"I'll have to look over everything and see if it would be a wise choice,"

"Look it over? What are you talking about? We both know that your business is going to burn out. I'm trying to save it," Victoria said, a bit snobby.

"If we go out of business, wouldn't that be better for your own?" Ruby chastised.

There was a pause for a few moments before they continued.

"As I said, I will go over the business plan and see if it would do the company any good," Ruby countered.

"What is there to go over?" Victoria snorted.

"I've heard for a while that your business is going under. You're just trying to save face," Ruby said.

"Listen here," Victoria shouted.

"You can leave," Ruby said as a dial tone sounded in the room.

"No need to get security involved. I'll see myself out,"

Suddenly, the door next to us opened and slammed shut. You could hear Victoria's footsteps as she stormed away from our location. I looked back over to Jasper, and he held his finger over his mouth for me to keep quiet.

The dial tone suddenly began to ring out as though a number had been dialed into the phone.

"Yes?" a male voice answered.

Suddenly, the voice disappeared, and the only thing we could hear was a one-way conversation.

"She came, just like you said," Ruby said.

She didn't say anything else and quickly hung up the phone. There was a slight sound of papers shuffling, followed by the sound of a light clicking off. I held my breath, hoping that she wouldn't be able to hear us breathing since we were able to hear her movements so clearly.

The sounds of a chair scraping across the floor startled me, but suddenly, we were able to hear Ruby's footsteps as she began toward the office door. The door opened and then shut, and we were able to hear her footsteps the entire way down the hall and even onto the stairs.

"Ready?" Jasper whispered.

I didn't say anything, just nodded in agreement.

Both of us exited the vacant space we had been occupying and stopped at the now-empty office. Jasper jiggled the door handle, but it didn't budge.

"Now what?" I asked as I peeked around to see if anybody had spotted us.

Luckily, nobody else was in the area.

"Now, I pick the lock," Jasper said.

"Where did you pick up that particular skill?" I laughed as I surveyed the area.

"That is a secret that you will never know,"

I continued to laugh but still looked around. I knew there wasn't anybody near, but I still wanted to keep a sharp lookout. After a few moments Jasper turned the door handle and pushed the office door open. I still couldn't shake the feeling that there were hundreds of eyes staring at us.

I walked into the office and headed over to the desk to turn the small light on. When I glanced around the room, there was a huge filing cabinet against a wall, and several paintings hung over it. There was a window that directly faced the door, so one could see outside as you entered and then have an even better view once you were seated at the desk. Everything else looked as it would in a normal business office. The odd thing was a rug in the center of the room that was a different color that didn't match the surrounding vicinity.

"Where do you think we should start looking?" Jasper whispered.

"Are you sure there aren't any cameras back here?" I asked.

"As far as I know, there wasn't anything installed. Nothing saying that there wasn't an update that I didn't get the memo on..." Jasper trailed on as he walked over to one of the filing cabinets.

I noticed there was a computer on the desk, and I began to click on the monitor. It wasn't password-protected, so I started to snoop through the system files.

"Is there a safe in the room?" I asked.

"I'm not sure. Why?"

"There is a file on the computer that states safe combination,"

I opened the file and began to write down the information. Once finished, I clicked off the computer and began to search the room. I walked over to each painting and slowly moved them to the side, just like in the movies.

Nothing.

"Has anything changed since the last time you were here?" I asked as I continued my investigation.

"Everything looks the same,"

A sudden idea popped into my head.

"What about this rug? There seems to be a slight noise discrepancy when you walk across the area," I said as I stepped onto the rug.

"It's always been there,"

"Will you help me with something?"

"Sure, what do you have in mind?"

"We need to move it slightly. I have a feeling I know where the safe is,"

We slowly moved the rug out of the way, and low and behold, the floor was different. Upon further examination, there was a slight catch on the floor, and when I moved it out of the way, the safe appeared.

"Did you say that you found the combination?"

"Yes, give me just a moment, and I'll have this opened,"

"I'll go take a quick peek to make sure that nobody has decided to make their way in our direction,"

"What are you going to do if somebody does make their way over here?" I laughed.

"I can be a great distraction," he replied while laughing.

I continued to input the safe's combination, and within a moment, it popped open. I struggled briefly since the door had to swing upward, but nevertheless, I was able to succeed in getting it fully open.

I glanced over in Jasper's direction, and when he caught my attention, he left his post and rushed over to see what I had discovered.

"What did you find?" he asked excitedly.

"I don't know. I haven't been able to look through anything yet,"

I rummaged through the safe and found a small envelope sitting at the very top; attached to it was an antique-looking key. I pulled both items out of the safe to fully examine them when suddenly the phone rang, startling us both. Jasper and I jumped but didn't dare to investigate further, so we shut the safe, ensured it was locked, and began to place everything back the way we had found it.

The phone stopped ringing, but my gut was telling me that we needed to get out of here. Without missing a beat, both Jasper and I headed out of the room and locked the door behind us. No sooner than we shut the door, we were able to hear footsteps coming back down the hallway. We rushed into the space we had occupied earlier to wait out the visitor.

We listened intently to the footsteps as they stopped right in front of the door. The handle jiggled, but the door never opened. I found it strange since Ruby obviously had a key.

Somebody else was trying to get into the office.

EIGHT

After a few tense minutes ticked by, I heard the same noise as when Jasper had been picking the lock. *Had this intruder decided to do the same thing we were just doing?*

Suddenly, the door clicked open, and heavy footsteps thudded into the room. Jasper tapped me urgently on the shoulder. His wide eyes and frantic gestures towards the door told me all I needed to know. I began to move, my heart pounding in my chest, inching my way toward the door, desperate not to make a sound that could give away our position.

"Where is it?" a gruff, menacing voice bellowed from within the room, the sound echoing off the walls.

My feet became rooted in their tracks, and I held my breath. Just as quickly as the noises came from the other side of the wall, they began to disappear. I was able to make out more shuffling, but it was headed back toward the door. Jasper had continued to try to nudge me, but I stayed firm. The door to the office slammed shut.

"Just great," the male voice said.

There was something oddly familiar about this voice, as though I had heard it before. I didn't have time to dwell on the thought of possibly knowing the intruder. I looked down at my hands and the weight from the key was slightly heavier than I would have anticipated. The envelope that was attached to it looked pristine from the outside.

The intruder stomped off down the hallway, and it felt like an eternity before I was brave enough to peek around the corner. Once satisfied that we were finally alone, the both of us slowly crept out of our hiding space.

"What do you think he was looking for?" I asked.

"I'm not sure. We didn't get a chance to look at everything inside the office. There would be no way for us to know if he took something," Jasper said.

I thought about his words and wondered if maybe we should hurry off with our forbidden treasure or continue to creep through the Bingo Haven. My mind must have already made the decision for me because, in an instant, I was already back on the stairs and making our way back down to the cleaning services crew. With any luck, the same crew that had cleaned up the rest of the mess would hopefully be on staff today.

"I take it that you're not done snooping for the day?" Jasper asked softly so only I could hear him.

"You would guess correctly,"

After we made our way through the inner knowing of the now-busy workplace, it was a bit harder for us to maneuver around. I saw a group of women getting their carts refilled with the necessary chemicals to clean the building before heading out for their shift.

"Excuse me," I said as I approached.

"Can I help you?" One of the women said as she walked away from her work cart.

"I was wondering, were any of you lovely ladies here on the night of the murder?" I asked.

"I was," she replied.

"Oh, good. I was wondering if you found anything around the crime scene that maybe the CSI workers might have missed?"

"I don't understand?"

"I was wondering if there was anything that you and your crew might have cleaned that the Police wouldn't have seen?"

"Oh, nothing that was missed on the inside of the building. The outside of the building, on the other hand,"

"What was missed on the outside?"

"Down at the loading dock, at the back of the building, there are several places where one bloody footprint was found as though it was pacing around,"

"The loading dock? I wasn't aware that this building had one?"

"Well, it's not officially owned by the BIngo Haven. It's in the building right next to ours. The only reason I know about this is because we have to take out the trash, and the dumpsters are located near the loading docks. I've seen a strange man with a hood and a hat on doing business down there. I don't like to go by myself at night,"

"Could you pick him out of a lineup if push comes to shove?"

"No, I'm sorry. I've never looked at the man directly, so I wouldn't have to make eye contact," she said as she bowed her head.

"I understand,"

"If you don't mind, I need to get back to my cart so I can get stocked before my shift,"

"Of course," I replied.

She walked back to the chemicals and other cleaning supplies and began to fully stock her cart. I walked away and was about to head outside to the loading dock.

"You're not going where I think you are? Are you?" Jasper questioned.

"Oh, now you decide to speak?"

"I didn't have anything that differed from what you were already asking. No need to confuse her with both of us asking," he chimed in.

"Fair point,"

"Again, you didn't answer my question,"

"Yes, I plan on going out to the docks. I don't think the investigators and the cleaning crew would have missed anything on the main bingo hall. A few days have passed since the incident, and you know more than one cleaning crew has passed through on shift. I think the best bet would be to check out back where apparently shady deals take place,"

"Fine, you're going to need your coat, though," Jasper said unhappily.

"I knew you would see it my way. Eventually," I laughed.

He didn't reply, just huffed slightly as both of us dressed to head outside into the cold day. We had worked our way through the working staff and made our way out back. When we emerged from the depth of the Bingo Haven, it felt as though the weather had changed entirely. I tried to find the sun, but just from guessing, I estimated that it had been a few hours since we had initially arrived.

"How long have we been inside?" I said out loud.

"By my guess, four hours," Jasper replied.

I hadn't expected an answer, but it surprised me nonetheless. I began to walk away from the warmth of the building and over to what looked like a full loading dock next door.

There were workers everywhere loading and unloading semi-trailers and moving the cargo into the building.

"I didn't know this was a full working business?" I muttered.

"Me either,"

I walked over to someone who looked like a foreman or at least somebody who was relatively in charge. He had his back turned to me, not paying attention to his surroundings.

"Excuse me?" I asked.

"Yes?" he said with the smell of alcohol on his breath.

I had to pause before I could reply. He definitely was a drinker, but he looked sober enough right now. He must have had several the night before.

"I was wondering what type of business this is?" I questioned.

"This is Cargo Needs, ma'am. This specific site is run by several others, and there are multiple locations across the state. Have you never seen us working before?" he questioned, his foul breath infiltrating my nostrils.

"No, sir. I haven't. Then again, I don't ever see any business coming from the front of the building. I don't usually see cars parked in the parking lot. The only ones I see are the spillover if the Bingo Haven happens to be busy. Have you guys been in business long?"

"Yes, we have been in business almost a full year at this location. Although the Cargo Needs company has been in business for many years,"

"Have you heard about what happened at the Bingo Haven?" Jasper asked.

"Yes, it was a tragedy. Losing a life is always tragic," the foreman replied.

"Has anybody washed the dock lately?" Jasper questioned.

"No," he answered with a quizzical look.

"Excellent," I noted.

"We're looking for something specific; we need permission to access the business. It could be vital for the investigation," Jasper added.

"The investigation? What are you, some kind of Police or something?"

"Let's go with or something," I noted.

"I can't let a couple of non-employees just wander around the facility looking for *clues*. If you want to search the property, you're going to need to come back with the real Police and a search warrant," the foreman gruffed before walking away.

Taking that as our cue to leave, both Jasper and I turned around and began to walk back to the rear entrance of the Bingo Haven. Neither of us spoke for several minutes.

"He does have a point, y'know," Jasper said, breaking the silence.

"I know he does. Still, it doesn't mean that we don't need to get in there. Do you think, with the information given, the Police would have enough to get a warrant?" I asked.

"No, most likely not. Even if they did, the crew is most likely going to destroy the evidence before we could do anything about it,"

What Jasper said made sense, but my next thought startled me.

"What if we go at night?"

"You mean breaking and entering?"

"I didn't say that; I just mean, what if we took a look around at nighttime?"

"That might work, as long as we don't get the Police called on us,"

"That would be an awkward conversation," I laughed.

We ducked inside the busy workplace and made our way through the unusually busy crowd and back out front into the cold air.

"The warmth was nice while it lasted,"

Jasper didn't reply as we headed to his truck. My stomach growled very unladylike.

"Where do you want to go grab a bite before we come back?"

"Since we do have several hours before nightfall, I would suggest we eat then separate to prepare for whatever tonight might bring,"

"Sounds fair. Are you going to grab a bite now or wait and order something later on?"

I thought about it briefly before I was unable to think of anywhere specific that I wanted to go.

"You pick; I'm not really in the mood for anything. So everything sounds good,"

"I have a feeling that you're going to regret this," he said while he climbed inside his truck.

For some odd reason, I did, too, although I was never going to let him know that. The truck soon roared to life, and then we were on our way to some unknown destination. From the route that Jasper was taking, I had a feeling of exactly where we were going.

"Please don't tell me," I said.

"You already know it. It's the best hole-in-the-wall joint around,"

"It's in the middle of a bowling alley,"

"I know that's why it's so great! Everybody knows about it, but their location really sucks. I think the only reason the bowling alley is still open is because of the business that the restaurant brings in,"

I did have to agree with Jasper. The location of *The Alley* restaurant really did suck, but the food was to die for. I loved how they have taken the food from simple cuisine to five-star quality. The problem was that so did everybody else, and we were never guaranteed a spot to sit right away. Sometimes, we were put on a waiting list.

"What are you going to get?" I asked.

"I don't know. I think I'm going to have to see if they anything on the daily special menu before scouring through the usual,"

"I know what you mean. At every place that we go to, I have something that I always stick to. I would like to try something new for a change,"

We pulled into the bowling alley's decrepit parking lot and rushed inside from the cold. As soon as we walked in, we were greeted by the usual workers for the bowling alley, but when we declined the proposition for a quick game, they moved on to the next guest who entered behind us.

We made our way over *to The Alley's* hostess station and waited our turn to be seated. It didn't take long, and we were quickly put into a booth at the back of the place. I kind of liked it, being back out of the way where nobody would pay me any attention. I could also listen in to the other conversations going on around me, as long as Jasper wouldn't keep me from breaking my concentration.

There was a group of three guys not too far from us; they were trying to speak in hushed tones. The waitress had been over to their table, and they just shooed her away. I thought it was odd, but shortly after that, the same waitress came over to our booth and began to take our drink order.

I could tell that she was super busy, as this was the usual lunch rush, but there seemed to be a shortage of front-of-the-house workers. The waitress returned with our drinks, and instead of being courageous with trying new foods, I stuck to my normal lunch, ultimate nachos with everything on it. I didn't even pay attention to what Jasper had ordered or what he and the waitress had spoken about.

The men who were not far from us still hadn't placed their drink order and continued to be gruff with the waitress.

"Hello?" Jasper said, waving a hand in front of my face.

"Sorry?" I replied.

"What are you doing?"

"Trying to listen," I said, gazing at the other table while straining to listen to their hushed voices.

"What do you want from me?" the first man asked.

"Keep your voice down," the second said.

"The incident at the Bingo Haven. Have you taken care of everything?" the first asked.

"I tried to go into the computer system and change some of the documents, but I think the Police already pulled them," the third said.

I was completely flabbergasted; these men were sitting here talking about what had happened at the Bingo Haven as though it wasn't an ordinary day.

"What about that, Lola or whatever?" the first asked.

"Did you do everything the boss said?" the second asked.

"Yes, right down to the..." he trailed off.

Down to the what?

"Good, we don't want the boss to be implicated, but if she keeps butting into our business, then we might have to take care of loose ends," the first said.

"Can we at least eat now?" the third griped.

"What about that Jasper character?" the second asked.

"The boss has something special planned for him. Once everybody knows his little secret. They will never trust him again," the first said as he picked up the menu.

Fear immediately gripped me at these men talking about my life as though it was nothing. I fumbled with my phone and tried to get pictures of them, but I wasn't any good at it. I looked over at Jasper, and his eyes were wide. The waitress soon returned with our food, and we ate as quickly as we could without attracting any attention to ourselves.

The men got the attention of our waitress and placed their orders just as we were leaving. She moved with such haste that I felt bad for her.

"Did you pay the bill?" I asked Jasper once we were out of range from the bad guys.

"I just left some money on the table to cover everything, including the tip. You can pay me back later," Jasper replied as we both hurried away from the scene.

NINE

With my senses officially on overdrive I wanted to stick around to get a better look at the bad guy's henchmen. Although something told me that it was an unwise choice given the information that just presented itself to me. I hurried away from The Alley's doors and headed over to Jasper's truck and waited for him to unlock it. Once we were both seated inside did, the weight of the situation hit me.

"We have to go to the shipping business tonight," I blurted out.

"You can't be serious. With what we just heard from those three scary guys? They could easily take us out," Jasper shrieked.

"That's exactly why we have to still stick to the plan,"

"I'm sorry, Lola, but I won't do it,"

"Fine,"

With me getting the last word, Jasper started his truck and began to head to my house. I couldn't wait to be alone so I could maybe think about how I was going to get myself into the warehouse. There had to be some sort of clues in there. Hopefully, there wasn't a night watchman or a security camera.

The trip back to my place was short, and I was glad that Jasper had decided not to stay. It was still a few hours until nightfall, and I was going to need to get some rest if I was going to go through with a half-cocked plan. Once I unlocked the door, Jasper drove off, and Jinx greeted me. After shutting the door and ensuring the locks were put back in place, I made my way over to the table. There was a large envelope sitting in the middle with my name written in rushed handwriting.

How did somebody get into my house? I didn't even touch it. I pulled out my cell phone and immediately dialed the Police Station's number and asked to be transferred to Officer James's line.

"This is James," the voice answered.

"This is Lola LaRue. You better come over; somebody has broken into my house and left me something on the table,"

"What is it?" he asked while papers shuffled in the background.

"It's an envelope, and it looks to be stuffed with something. I haven't opened it. I just got home, and I made sure that all of the windows and the doors were locked before I left,"

"Don't go anywhere. I'll be right over," he said before the line disconnected.

I didn't want to sit around inside the house waiting for somebody to possibly attack me. I went and stood by the front door, ready to bolt if necessary. I couldn't help but keep an eye on my watch to count the minutes until Officer James would arrive.

Seven dreadful minutes ticked by until I saw the lights flashing on the top of two cars. Both Officer James and Franks jumped out of their cars and rushed to my door. I opened it and allowed both men to enter the house.

"Stay outside with the other Officers until we can secure the house,"

I rushed outside toward the other two Officers who were just getting out of their vehicle. Neither of them said anything as they waited for their brothers-in-arms to secure my home.

Time seemed to drag on as the three of us waited for the call to come through the walkie-talkie.

"House is secured, everybody is good to go," Officer James' voice said.

I rushed toward the front door when something caught my attention in my flower garden. Usually, in the spring and summer, I would put out gnomes and other ornaments. I had taken them down and put them away since winter was pretty much here. There was a colorful gnome sitting right beside my front porch step. It was odd because I had never seen it before, and it didn't belong to me.

"Wait," I said to the two unknown-named Officers.

I bent down to look at the gnome, which was holding a sunflower, and it looked like it would have been solar-powered, except there wasn't any place for a light to be on it.

"I want to snap some pictures of the envelope and dust around the area for any prints," Officer James said.

"You might want to take this back with you too for more evidence,"

"Isn't that yours?" Officer Franks asked.

"No, I already put mine away for the season. I haven't been paying too much attention to my house surroundings, so I'm unsure when this could have arrived," I said.

"Is that a camera?" Officer Franks asked.

"I'm not sure. I've never seen anything like it before,"

"We'll bag and tag it for evidence. Whoever is doing this is going through a lot of trouble to intimidate you,"

He walked back up with an evidence kit bag, placed it in a large bag, sealed it tight, and began to initial and date it.

"You said you never opened the envelope?" Officer Franks asked in a softer tone.

I was taken aback by the softness in his voice, as though this was something more personal for him.

"No, I never touched it," I replied.

"We need to open it and see what's inside," Officer James said.

I nodded in agreement and walked back inside the house toward the envelope. From the kit that Officer James brought, Officer Franks grabbed the camera and began to take photos of the area and began to take measurements for the official case report. With gloves on, Officer James grabbed hold of the manilla envelope and slowly opened it by the fastener on the back.

I was completely in shock because it was mostly pictures of me in various places. All of them most recently. Jasper was in a few of them, but some were from the Bingo Haven's Office with me breaking into the safe. There were even shots of me entering and exiting my home.

"Is somebody trying to blackmail me?" I asked with a bit of fear.

"We will take this back to the lab and have them process everything," Officer James said as he placed the images back inside the envelope before placing the entire thing in an evidence bag. "I want you placed in protective custody immediately,"

"No, I will not be bounced around from safe house to safe house while others are trying to figure out what is going on," I said.

"You will have a set of uniforms stationed outside your home then," Office Franks said, agreeing with Officer James.

How was I going to get into the warehouse now?

Sighing in defeat, I nodded in agreement with both of them. I wasn't sure how somebody was getting into my home while it was still locked.

"Fine, I'll order in for the night. I have somebody coming over tomorrow to fix my window, which was broken a few days ago,"

"Since we are all agreed, let us finish up in here. Can you take a look around and see if there is anything out of place or added to the house that might be a camera?" Officer Franks asked.

"Yeah, I can do that," I sighed.

I left the Officers to do their work and began to investigate each and every room for anything that might be out of place or simply added to my collection of knick-knacks.

I started near my bedroom and looked for any possible angle at which a microphone or camera could be hidden. I didn't have too many breakables in the house. I didn't like to pick them up and move them around to dust. I hated to dust.

I looked around at three different figurines, and something near a mirror caught my attention. There was an added figure of a kitten and puppy playing together that I hadn't placed there.

I picked it up and it was heavier than it originally looked. I examined the space it was in, and I couldn't help but notice the dust underneath it. Somebody had placed it there recently. I went back toward the kitchen and placed the object on the counter, then quickly went back to my search.

I found a total of five other figurines that weren't mine, and they, too, had dust underneath them. I placed the rest of the figurines next to the original one.

"None of these cute little figures are mine," I said as the Officers were finishing up.

"Do you have a spare key that you keep outside?" Officer James asked.

A lightbulb went off inside me, and I suddenly knew how the bad guys were getting in.

"Yes," I replied.

"Can you go and get it?" Officer Franks asked.

I left the Officers to finish up their work as I quickly walked outside to look for the fake rock that held my house key. I found it, not in its usual spot, and when I opened it, there wasn't a key inside it.

"Great," I said as I walked back inside with my empty rock.

"Is the key still there?" Officer Franks asked.

"No. Although, somehow, I think you already knew that," I replied.

"Call it a gut feeling," Officer Franks said.

His demeanor caught me off guard because he was actually being friendly, as though somebody had a stern talking with him about manners and other human emotions.

"Can I talk to you?" Officer Franks asked, nudging me to the side.

I followed him to my living room to hear what he had to say.

"I wanted to apologize. My Mom gave me a good tongue-lashing about my mannerisms and kindness toward others. She reminded me why I wanted to be an Officer. My Mother also wanted me to thank you for always helping my sister every time she came into the library,"

I was completely taken aback.

"Apology accepted, and you're welcome,"

We both shared a moment together, and I knew that the man who had been abrupt with me before would no longer rear its ugly face.

"Now that you guys have had a wonderful moment, Lola, we're going to take all this evidence to the lab and have it analyzed. It might take a few days, but there will always be a set of uniforms stationed outside of the house. If you plan on leaving, you must inform them where you're going so they can follow you. I've already informed the first set of uniformed Officers that you have a repair guy going to be here tomorrow morning. They should alert their reliefs and so on. Now, I'm going to be off tomorrow, but Officer Franks will still be on duty. If you can think of anything, just call," Officer James said.

"Or if you need somebody just to talk to, you can call too," Officer Franks added.

"Thank you," I said to all of them.

They gathered up all of their stuff and left the house; both cars remained in my driveway until a third car pulled up. Officer James got out of his car and talked to the third car that had arrived.

After Officer James and the occupants of the third car were finished talking, they drove away and returned within seconds to pull into my driveway. The first two cars left, and the third one was parked in their spots. If I were to try and sneak away, they would undoubtedly report me to their superiors, and I don't want my lead to get spooked. I would just need to bide my time for now.

I walked away from the window and went to get the takeout menus to decide what Jinx and I would have for dinner. The lunch that I had eaten earlier had completely worn through me, and I was hungry again. Knowing it was still early for dinner, I decided to order in early tonight.

"Jinx, what would you like tonight?" I asked out loud.

She came from her hiding spot and jumped onto the stand from which I had pulled the menus. She walked over all of them but sat on top of the one with specialty pizza.

"I see. Pizza?" I asked.

She mewed in response, and I walked outside to the Officers.

"Is there something we can help you with?" two men asked.

"I was just about to order some pizza for dinner; I was wondering if you would like anything?" I asked.

They both looked surprised by my offer.

"No, thank you. Although, when you are done ordering, we could use the menu,"

"We could order on one, and then you guys can pay me back later," I replied.

"Alright, makes sense," they agreed.

"Go ahead and write down what you two would like, and I'll order it. I'm going to have it delivered,"

"We will check the order once it arrives for safety," one man said.

"I wouldn't expect it any other way,"

They both had written down what they wanted and handed over a piece of paper.

"Would you guys like to come inside and out of the cold? It has to be painful sitting in the car the entire time?" I asked.

"That sounds amazing. We'll be in when the pizza arrives,"

"I'll head in and order it now,"

I headed back in from the cold and looked over the menu to see what I wanted for the night. Once satisfied with my choices, I called the restaurant and ordered the food. I ensured that I gathered the total and the estimated time.

Once completed, I headed into the living room to sit in my chair and try to unwind for the night. The thought of somebody having my house key unnerved me, and I needed to get in touch with a locksmith to change the locks on the house.

I shut my eyes to try and clear the thoughts from my head, but soon, there was a knock on the door. I peeked out the window, and I saw the Officer's car was turned off. I got up from my chair and opened the door to the two smiling men holding our food.

"We can't say thank you enough for allowing us to come in and be able to sit down and eat. It's a lot more comfortable at a table rather than inside a car," the first said.

"It's my pleasure. I wouldn't want anybody to be uncomfortable. Please follow me to the kitchen so we can get started," I said with a smile.

I had this gut feeling that I knew both of these men. Maybe they frequented the library when I worked there. I led them through my small house and into the kitchen. I grabbed some plates and offered drinks, but both asked for water.

After the pleasantries were over, the two men began to relax, and that was when it hit me. These men were children, and I helped their Mothers in the library. I would assist them with job searches or whatever else they needed from the computers.

"Do you remember us?" the first man asked in between bites of food.

"I do. Although, I'm sorry to say that I don't recall your names," I replied.

"I am Mike Abdul, and this is my best friend and co-worker, Sasha Verez,"

"You would help our Mothers and also keep us out of trouble while they hunted for jobs and state help," Sasha said.

"Yes, I remember multiple times that you two were thick as thieves and fell asleep in my arms more than once. I offered to give your Mother's a break while they tried to look for items they needed. They took me up on it a couple of times," I said after a mouthful of pizza.

TEN

After we finished eating, we cleaned up the kitchen area, and the two young men were about to head back to their patrol car.

"Is there anything else you need before we head back out?" Officer Abdul asked.

"I think that is everything. I'm getting ready to head to bed for the night. Thank you for the lovely company and reminiscing about the past," I said.

"In the morning, there should be a different set of Officers posted outside. If everything isn't settled by tomorrow night, then we will be back on duty," Officer Sasha said.

"Thank you again; good night," I said while walking them toward the front door.

They took the trash out with them, and I watched from the front door as they entered their car. They then began to write up some reports. I shut and locked the door behind me and headed to the bathroom to start getting ready for the evening. There was a sudden ringing on the phone, and I shut the running water from the sink off and rushed to answer it.

"Hello?" I answered.

"Hello, Miss. Lola?"

"Yes, this is her,"

"It's Alan. I'm just confirming that it's still ok for me to come over tomorrow morning to start the work on the window,"

"Yes. I'll be expecting you around eight in the morning,"

"Sorry for calling so late. See you then,"

I hung up the phone, went back to the bathroom, and continued the regiment of washing my face. Once satisfied that I had washed the grime away, I went to the bedroom and finished getting ready to bed. I laid down, closed my eyes, and waited for sleep to come.

THE NEXT MORNING, I awoke at around seven o'clock to start getting ready for the day. I showered quickly and got dressed in the bathroom, just in case I missed any knick-knacks yesterday.

I had just finished getting ready for the day when there was a knock at my front door. I looked through the peephole, and it was Jasper. He must have gotten over the small disagreement from yesterday.

I opened the door and allowed him to come in.

"Do you know that there is a Police car sitting in your driveway?" he asked with shock.

"Yes, I do know this,"

"Did something happen yesterday after I dropped you off?" he questioned.

"Yes, I called the Police Station and had Officers come over to investigate the envelope that was sitting on my kitchen table," I noted with a hint of annoyance.

"Why didn't you call me?" he asked with a bit of hurt written in his eyes.

"Jasper, you and I have been over this more than once. We are not dating, and I don't need to call you for everything. In fact, why is it that you're here this early in the morning?"

"You told me that Alan was going to be here to fix the window," he said.

"Yes, and I'm perfectly capable of being by myself while a repairman is here," I scolded him.

"I just didn't think that you should be by yourself," he mumbled.

"I think you should leave,"

"What?"

"You have overstepped your boundaries, and I've had enough of your foolishness. Now, please, leave,"

With hurt written in his posture, he walked back to the front door and looked back briefly before leaving without saying another word.

Jinx strolled out of the bedroom and mewed at me for breakfast.

"Jinx, what has gotten into that man?" I questioned out loud.

I left the door and walked into the kitchen, about to make a pot of coffee, when there was another knock on the door.

"This better not be Jasper again," I hissed.

I opened the door expecting Jasper's figure to be standing on my front stoop, but instead, it was a man that I had never met before.

"May I help you?" I asked the gentleman.

"I hate to be intruding, but I'm new to the neighborhood, and I was going around the area and introducing myself. My name is Arthur Pennington. I moved from Sterling Ridge," the man introduced himself.

"My name is Lola LaRue, and I was the local librarian here in town, well, at least before retirement, of course," I laughed.

"I couldn't help but notice that the Police have been stationed outside of your house all night. May I ask if everything is alright? I know that you just met me..." he trailed off.

"I'm hoping so. There have been a few things going on around town, and somehow, I ended up in the middle of it," I mused.

"Sounds like something I just moved away from," he commented.

"You don't say,"

"I ended up solving a murder from my hometown and stopped a serial arson,"

"Would you care to come in?" I asked, gesturing toward the house.

"I'm sorry?"

"I was hoping that we could speak more of your adventure, and maybe you might be able to give me some pointers on my personal ordeal," I confessed.

"I appreciate the offer, but I'm not really in the mood to speak about the past today. Maybe we could grab a bite to eat in a few days, just as friends?"

"That sounds lovely. I'm sorry for putting you on the spot,"

"I was just taken aback. That's all. I'll get in touch with you in a few days about my story,"

"Talk to you then,"

I was about to shut the door when Alan's truck pulled up to the curb. He sat in the truck momentarily, then quickly got out and rushed to the door.

"Lola!"

"You're a little early," I smiled.

"I wanted to let you know that you're going to need to shut the heat off to the house, and you might want to put on some extra layers. I'm going to be taking off the plywood that I had hung the other day. It's going to get cold really quick in the house,"

"Oh, I see." I hadn't really thought about what it would mean to have someone fix a hole in my house.

"Let me go ahead and get more layers on and turn off the heat to the house,"

I watched as Alan walked back to his truck to begin unloading the supplies that he would need to complete the job. I left the front door, headed to the thermostat, switched it off, and then went to get my coat on. I knew that I didn't need it yet, but soon, it would be extremely cold in the house. Jinx mewed happily around my feet as I went to the kitchen to get a cup of coffee when I suddenly remembered that I never started a pot for the morning.

Groaning to myself, I quickly started the pot and went to wait in the living room. I heard construction noises coming from the kitchen area, and I picked up one of my books to try to take everything off my mind and get lost in the characters' world.

I was able to read one chapter before the sudden silence filled my home. I set down my book and got up from my chair to look around. The window was only halfway put in. There seemed to be several items missing, and a cold breeze was still roaming through the house.

"Alan?" I called out.

Two Officers busted through the door and began to do a sweep of the house.

"Lola, I need you to back away from the window," a female Officer said.

I did as she instructed and quickly headed back to the living room. I glanced out of the front window to see what would have caused them to rush into the house.

"The house is clear; I'm going to go check the back area," the second Officer said.

"Copy, I'll stay put,"

"What is going on?"

"Call it a hunch," she said.

"Back here, the worker has been injured, and he's unconscious on the ground. He's bleeding. Call 911!" the male Officer shouted.

The female Officer pulled out a radio and called 911 to my address.

It took them three minutes to get to the house, and the male Officer outside directed them to where Alan was. I walked to the kitchen so I could listen in.

"Sir, do you know what happened?" the first paramedic asked.

"No?" he muttered.

"Do you know your name?"

The second paramedic began to take vitals and assess the situation. He grabbed gauze and began to treat the wound.

"Sir, we believe you were attacked," the male Officer noted.

"Attacked?" Alan asked, confused.

"What do you remember what happened before you were attacked?" the male Officer asked.

"I was working on replacing Lola's window, and I turned around to get more material, and then there was a pain at the back of my head," he said as he tried to sit up.

"Sir, I don't advise you to move just yet. We are still wrapping the wound, and I can tell there is a giant goose egg where the open wound is. I haven't been able to assess the damage done yet. You might need to go to the hospital and have a few stitches placed,"

"What? I have to finish this job. I can't let this window stay open," Alan protested.

"Why don't you just put the plywood over the window again and head to the hospital to get checked out. You can come back tomorrow and finish if you're able to," I said.

"Alright," Alan said as he began to slowly sit up with the help of the paramedics. "It will only take a few screws and it will be covered back up,"

Alan quickly did the work and then agreed to be taken to the hospital to be looked at. The Officers asked me a slew of questions to see if I knew anything, and I didn't. When they were satisfied with my answers, they went back to their patrol car, and I watched as they began to write up some reports.

I went and turned the heat back on and headed back to my chair to start reading again.

My cell began to ring and it brought me from the book world back to reality. At the same time, there was a knock on my door, and when I glanced at the time, I couldn't believe several hours had passed. I didn't bother to head to the phone; if it was important, they could leave me a message.

I opened the door, and Arthur Pennington was waiting in the cold.

"Hello? I thought I wouldn't be seeing you for a few days," I said as I opened the door.

"I heard about the attack on your worker friend earlier today. The paramedics were needed and everything. Do you mind if I come in out of the cold?" he asked.

"Sure," I gestured into the house.

"I wasn't going to stop by, but I think that we need to talk sooner rather than later," he admitted.

"I was about to make some dinner if you would like some?" I offered.

"My story is long, and it might take some time to go through it all. Dinner would be lovely,"

"Sorry that there is still a chill in the air, but you might want to keep your coat on for a little while. At least until you adjust," I laughed and headed to the kitchen.

"That's alright. From what I was able to gather, you had an accident, and somehow your window was damaged?"

"Actually, I'm not sure what happened. I woke up, and my cat was gone, and it was cold outside. My friend Jasper found her wandering down the street. Luckily, she is very accustomed to him, and she ran toward him for a quick and easy rescue. As for my window, I thought that it was just a neighborhood kid," I said as I began to get some pork chops from the fridge, which I had luckily laid out earlier in the day.

I only half remember actually laying out the meat, but it was a good thing that I did. I wasn't sure I could eat another meal out.

"Do you mind if I sit while you cook? We only just met, and I don't want to do anything unwelcoming," Arthur asked.

"I'm a pretty friendly person, and seeing as my kitchen is not that big, I think I will be able to hear you from the stove. That is if you don't mind talking while I cook?" I asked.

"I can work with that," he smiled.

I began to get out the ingredients so I could make a mixture of breading so I could begin to fry the meat. I also grabbed a can of vegetables and began to make a small batch of cornbread.

"Let me start with a little bit of background. I was a barber in my hometown of Sterling Ridge. I knew everybody, and everybody knew me. It's also a small town, so it was easy to do. My real passion is taking care of and sculpting bonsai trees. I know it's an odd hobby, but I really enjoy it. I was living my mundane life, the same thing every day, and then there was a fire at the historic Sterling Ridge Inn. I was walking home when I saw it being engulfed in flames, and the fire department rushed to the rescue. For some reason, I was pulled to the scene, and I learned that one of the patrons who frequented the Inn due to fights with his spouse had died in the fire. I initially hadn't thought anything of it, but there was this nagging feeling in the pit of my stomach. Time went on after the funeral, and the news that the fire had been started on purpose and the possibility of murder was in the air, I had to begin my own investigation. I'm not sure what pulled me to it, if it was for the loss of one of the usual patrons in town or if it was the second fire that was more serious than the first. Whatever it was, I was hooked. I went to my local Police Station and began to ask simple questions, started my own list of clues, and began to investigate people on the down low. After all, I was the town barber; everybody would come to me for a haircut. It was also a great way for me to get the gossip of the town," he paused.

I was intently listening while I cooked.

"So far, we sound to be in the same situation," I said while pulling a few pork chops from the pan.

"Everybody had secrets in the town that would slip when they spoke to a friend. I also found out that many suspected the wife of the fire victim, but that was too easy. I looked at who would gain the most from both fires in town, and only one name stuck out. Clara Benson was a local antique shop owner who was going to buy into the Inn due to financial strain on the other owners, but they turned her down because she wanted to take several antiques from the Inn and put them in her shop. She was secretly selling them to a higher class who would pay top dollar for the items,"

I was plating up the food, and I walked over to the table to set out the small dinner that I had made. I went to grab a few bottles of water for us to drink.

"I'm sorry, I don't have anything fancy to offer," I said as I wiped my hands on a dish towel.

"No worries,"

"Let me tell you about my situation,"

ELEVEN

By the time I had finished telling Arthur everything that had happened over the last few days he sat back in his chair and contemplated my words.

"It does seem that you're in quite a predicament," he mused.

"May I be honest?" I asked.

"You just told a complete stranger your entire ordeal; I think you have earned the right to be honest,"

"I feel so connected to you for some really odd reason. Call me crazy, but it seems that our paths might have crossed for some reason. Someone else going through something so similar is so strange. It feels surreal," I said.

"It is odd that I find myself immersed in another mystery. I've always had a knack for finding out the truth," he smiled.

"I sound like a total fool," I laughed.

I got up from my seat, put away a few leftovers, and started to clean the dishes. Arthur got up and handed me his plate and leaned against the counter.

"No. Well, to anyone else, yes, you would sound like a fool. But to me, it sounds like any other day," he laughed.

I took the plate from his hands and thought about his words. We stood in silence for a few minutes, both of us not daring to interrupt the easy friendship that had just formed.

"I'm glad you stopped by tonight. I really needed some company after what happened earlier,"

"It was my pleasure. I also think that you should get into that warehouse and see what that company might be hiding," he said as he crossed his arms.

"You do?"

"Absolutely. I might have done the same thing to a place or two,"

"I had almost put those plans behind me. I'm not sure how I'm going to get out of here with the Officers sitting outside my home,"

"Just go to the Bingo Haven as though you were going to play for a few hours," Arthur insisted.

"What?"

"It's not that complicated. The Officers will stay here knowing that you're going to a place that has security roaming around at every corner,"

"What do you mean security?" I asked.

"I went there earlier today, and there were at least five Officers roaming around the building. When I asked for more information, they blew me off as if I was a nobody,"

"That doesn't sound like the Officers around here. Most everybody is friendly,"

"I don't think they were real Officers. I think they were imposters there to guard something,"

"Or guard something that they don't already know was taken?" I said.

"What do you mean guard something that they don't know was already taken. Did you steal something?"

"I didn't steal it, I'm just borrowing it,"

I quickly stopped what I was doing and went to get the key from my purse. When I returned, I handed it over with ease so he could examine it.

"This looks like it would open some kind of old lock. Like an antique or something. I've never seen anything like it. Where did you find it?"

"I sort of found it locked inside a safe in the office of the Bingo Haven,"

"I wonder what this would unlock?"

There was a sudden noise from the living room of something crashing onto the floor. I couldn't help but jump and rush to make sure Jinx was ok.

"Oh, Jinx, look what you've done," I laughed.

She had knocked over the book that I had been reading, Black Bear Alibi. I picked it back up and set it on my chair, and wandered back into the kitchen.

"I always thought that when the Police were watching your home that, you were kind of on like house arrest?" I admitted.

"No, they can't technically make you stay without probable cause, or you actually have a house monitor on. Since I'm guessing they don't have either on you..."

Arthur handed back the key and I handled it with care. I turned it over once to examine the intricate details that were etched into the metal.

"I hate to overstay my welcome, but I think that I should be heading home. I know it's not very far, but it looks like you have quite a few things on your mind,"

"I understand completely. Again, thank you for coming over and listening to my tale. Maybe someday you can go into more detail about what happened with you and your situation?"

"Someday," he said as he began to make his way toward the door.

I walked him to the door and locked it once he had left the threshold. I didn't watch him through the window as I was sure with the Officers sitting outside my home, he would make it back safely.

The days were starting to blur together, and my normal sense of peace was starting to fray at the tense edges. I felt sorry for Tom's family, who will bury their family member with unsure answers.

There was still the forensic report noting that somebody was using the Bingo Haven as a front to launder money. Somebody wanted me to take the fall for the murder and is still threatening my presence within the area.

I sighed slightly and rubbed my temples in the hope that the headache that had suddenly formed would go away. I finished the nightly stuff that needed to be done before I headed to bed. I didn't look at the time, for I wasn't sure I truly wanted to know how late I might stay up and ponder the thoughts that plagued me.

I went to the bedroom and laid down, and prayed that the intrusive thoughts would stay away.

I AWOKE EARLY the next morning with last night's thoughts still roaming in my mind. I got ready for the day and went to inspect my home. Not that I was expecting anything to be amiss, but there was this nagging feeling that wouldn't go away.

I felt that Arthur was right. I had all but put away the thought of going through with my plan, but after hearing part of his tale, I changed my mind. I peeked over at the clock once I decided to make a pot of coffee; it was six o'clock in the morning. I sighed internally, knowing it was going to be at least a few hours before the Bingo Haven opened.

I went over to my chair and picked up my book to pass the time.

Within moments, I could smell the coffee, and after a while, I set the book down to get my first cup of the day. Once satisfied, I headed back to my chair and began to read again.

Being in the world of my characters really made the time pass, when there was a sudden knock on the door. I pulled myself away from the story and peeked out the window. Jasper's red truck sat on the street.

I went to the door and opened it before Jasper could knock again.

"Hi, Lola," he said.

"Hello, Jasper,"

"I was on my way to the Bingo Haven for my shift, and I was wondering if you wanted to go for a while? Maybe play a few rounds and try to put some of what's happening behind us?" he asked.

"I guess this is your way of apologizing?"

"Yes,"

"Let me grab my things, and I'll be out in a few. If you want, you can wait in your truck, and I'll be right there,"

I shut the door, not waiting for his response, and quickly went to get my purse and my coat. I went outside and held my coat together through the chill that tried to bite through my coat. I bypassed the Officers who were sitting in their car and headed straight for Jasper's truck.

I opened the door and quickly shut it behind me, trying to keep the warmth in the cab. Jasper didn't say anything; just waited patiently for me to get comfortable, and then headed toward the Bingo Haven.

Neither of us was willing to break the silence in the cab. I looked out of the windshield and watched as the snow began to fall. First, it was slow; there was just a snowflake here and there. Then, it was more frequent.

"The roads will probably be worse on the way home. Just a thought in case you want to swing by anywhere afterward. Don't want to get snowed in or anything," he said tensely.

So much for that apology, I thought to myself.

"Thank you for the thought; I'll keep that in mind for when we leave,"

"My shift might not be for as long as usual since it's starting to snow. I heard that we're supposed to get a blizzard or something similar to major snowfall,"

"I haven't watched the news lately, I've been preoccupied,"

"Are you going to be hanging out in your usual spot?"

"I've got some business to handle before I play a few rounds,"

"Just be careful whatever you do,"

Jasper pulled into the parking lot, and the snow began to come down harder. I got out of the truck and hurried inside to bite the cold. I waited inside the threshold of the business while Jasper slowly walked inside.

"I thought you didn't like the cold?" I laughed.

"It just doesn't bother me today as much as it usually does," he admitted.

Both of us walked away from the entrance and then parted ways. He went toward the back employee room to put his coat and belongings away, and I walked through the morning shift, bustling about to the back entrance.

During my walkthrough I saw three people who wore Officer's uniforms, but I had never seen any of them before. Although I didn't know the entire force, and they could be on loan from another department, I still found it odd for them to be here.

I had almost made it to the back of the building and into the cold again before I was stopped by the fourth Officer.

"Excuse me, ma'am?" he said.

"Me?" I stuttered.

"Nobody should be back here. All of the employees were told that this has now become a restricted area,"

"I'm sorry. I didn't get the memo. I'm filling in for someone, and I usually don't work too many hours," I lied.

"I understand, but you still can't be back here," he said.

"Alright," I said as I walked back to the bustling of the other employees.

"What were you doing back here anyway?" he asked.

"My co-worker said that she left some cleaning equipment at the dumpsters and asked for me to go and get them before they were mistaken for the trash," I lied.

The Officer stood for a moment as though he was trying to see if I had been telling the truth. I didn't waver in my stance and was about to turn around and find another way to the warehouse.

"Wait. Just don't be too long. It's getting cold out there," he said, turning away from me and headed in another direction.

"Thank you," I said to his back.

He didn't respond; he just continued on his path toward a dark corridor. I headed outside, and the cold hit me in the face, but I wasn't prepared for the shadows cast by the building, making it colder.

As soon as I walked outside, I waited momentarily to listen for the hustle and bustle of the warehouse workers, except there weren't any. I took this as a good sign and quickly walked over to the back of the building.

I found the door that would lead into the heart of the warehouse and jiggled the handle. It was unlocked. I opened it slightly and peeked inside to again listen for the sounds of the crew to begin their work day. Still nothing.

I walked in, and it wasn't what I really expected. There was nothing on the inside of the building to suggest there were ever any workers there. There were no schedules hanging or anything personal on the desks that I found near a wall.

What if it had been all for show?

I continued to walk around and finally found a peg board with a general schedule. Upon further investigation, I found that all of the workers were supposed to be scheduled off for today. Good.

This would give me ample time to look around the facility without anybody interrupting me. I tried to open the door to the office, but it was locked. I walked around and found some empty crates, all busted open from the top. The crates were something that would have been moved from semi-trucks. I went to one of the opened boxes to sift around to see if I was able to find anything. Nothing.

I looked around for a shipping manifest and still came up empty-handed. I saw several rooms and tried to open each of them, and to my surprise, they opened. I came up to one room that was locked, and I was about to turn away when something kept nagging in the back of my mind. I turned back around and found a key hanging on the wall. Why didn't I see this the first time?

I grabbed the key from the wall and slid it into the keyhole, and unlocked the door with ease. Upon opening the door, I immediately saw several bingo items placed haphazardly in every opening.

This doesn't make any sense. Why would a shipping company have so many bingo items strung around like they were being stolen? What if this is part of the front? Putting out bingo items for the real intake. The hidden money that was found on the ledger.

I didn't bother trying to find anything else within the building. I hoped that there weren't any security cameras that would have caught me snooping around. I also needed to get back into the Bingo Haven before anybody noticed me missing.

I left the same way I had entered and made sure nobody was watching. I didn't find any clues as to who would have been behind the money laundering or any type of lock that would have fit the key that I borrowed. I was going to need to dig deeper.

I re-entered the Bingo Haven and made my way to where Jasper had been calling out numbers. It seemed as though he hadn't been up there for very long or maybe he had and wasn't really paying too much attention to his surroundings. It was as though the spark that he usually had wasn't there today. I would need to ask him what was going on later.

"May I have your attention, please," a male voice said over the intercom. "The Bingo Haven will be closing shortly due to the severe weather that is supposed to be here in a few hours. We appreciate your business, and we will announce the reopening after the storm has passed,"

Odd.

I didn't buy any cards to play; I just sat in the back and waited for Jasper to finish his early shift. I had a feeling that he knew more than his facial expression was willing to tell.

"Are you waiting for me?" Jasper asked a short while later.

"You are my mode of transportation," I gently reminded him.

"Oh, right. Did you decide if you needed to stop anywhere before I take you back to your place?"

"No, I think I'm alright. I do have other questions,"

"Not here," he whispered.

We left the establishment and there was at least three inches of snow that covered the entire area. The few who had braved the weather were also getting in their vehicles. I saw several other workers doing the same. After we were safe in Jasper's truck, I began to ask a slew of questions.

"What's really going on?" I berated him.

"I can't tell you,"

"Can't or won't?"

"The owner of the facility wants to complete a thorough inventory as there have been some discrepancies in the books. According to the email sent, he is not happy with how the establishment has been handled, and there might be people not returning to work in a few days,"

"Did the email say anything else?"

"No,"

TWELVE

I stewed on the information that Jasper had just presented to me. I always knew that there might have been someone higher up on the food chain who owned the business. Although Ruby was always a great manager, and I had always heard great praise from the usual hustle and bustle of the crew doing their jobs. It made me sit back and think of what was happening within the business.

I mean, I wasn't on the need to know everything that happened within the walls of the Bingo Haven, but Jasper was, or he at least pretended not to be. He only worked one to two days a week, just enough to keep retirement from being boring.

"Jasper, are you heading anywhere in particular?" I asked.

"Just heading to drop you off,"

"Can we make a pit stop?"

"Where did you have in mind? Something to eat?"

"No, at least that's not what's on my mind,"

"Alright, where to then?"

"Vixen's Bingo Palace,"

"You want me to take you to my company's rival business?"

"Yes,"

"I've always tried to imagine what goes through your mind, but I'm not even going to try this time,"

He changed direction, and it felt like we were there in a heartbeat. Once Jasper parked, I quickly headed toward the inside of the building before the snow could bury me. It had really picked up during our drive over. I looked back and noticed that Jasper hadn't gotten out of the truck. I guess he was going to sit this one out.

When I went inside and Victoria was talking with one of her employees. The younger girl was almost in tears from the heated conversation between the two. I was hoping to catch her not in a foul mood, but I at least waited until they were finished before I began to approach her.

"Victoria!" I said, voice slightly raised to get her attention.

She had been walking away from the conversation with her employee when she changed directions and headed toward me.

"Lola. What a surprise. What can I do for you?" she asked.

"I actually wanted to talk about a few things. Do you have a few minutes?"

She nodded her head in agreement, headed toward the cafe part of the business, and sat down at one of the vacant tables.

"What is it you wanted to talk about?"

"Well, to be honest, this was a spur-of-the-moment thing. I can clearly see that since the incident at the Bingo Haven, you seem to have drummed up more business for yourself,"

"That's true,"

"I also heard a rumor that you wanted the Bingo Haven to be partners with your establishment. Although they turned that offer down,"

"The rumor is true,"

"I just can't help but wonder why they would want to turn it down. I'm pretty sure that there would have been a few minor details that needed to be worked out, but they would have had control over both of the Bingo places in the area. What could their motive be?"

Victoria didn't say anything at first, and she ordered coffee when

I was ranting. She stayed quiet until she took a long drink from her cup.

"I'll be honest with you, Lola, I don't know their motives. I've mainly dealt with Ruby, but one other time, I met with the actual business owner. I like to call him Mr. Mysterious because he never actually introduced himself,"

"What was he like?"

"You could tell that he is used to getting his way. He is a bit on the larger side, but his suit was well-made for him. He talked business in a way that I'm unfamiliar with. He brushed off my attempts back then just as he is now,"

"I've never had the pleasure to meet this Mr. Mysterious,"

"I'm not sure you would want to. Like I said, he was well diverse in the business world, but his mannerisms lacked any type of niceties,"

"I'll keep that in mind. Thank you, Victoria,"

"Why are you asking so many questions?"

"Let's just say there have been too many things that are not adding up in the case,"

"I wish you luck, Lola,"

She finished her coffee and then headed toward the kitchen staff. I got up myself and headed back toward Jasper's truck. I looked at all of the sweepstakes decor that was strung around the business and laughed on the inside. *If Victoria's business has been going under for a few years, how is she able to afford to send winners away on vacations?*

This new question immediately was followed up by a few more. *Who was sponsoring these trips? Where did she find sponsors knowing that the business is going under? Was Victoria Smith involved in money laundering to ensure her business thrived?*

I hadn't been inside very long, but the snow had started to come down in blizzard conditions. I rushed back to the truck, which was running, and Jasper had a sour look on his face.

"What?" I questioned.

"Why did you want to come here?"

"Well, if you would have given me a moment, I would have told you,"

He didn't reply, but the look on his face softened a little. He put the truck in gear, and we headed back down the road toward the neighborhood in which we shared.

"I talked with Victoria and asked her a few questions about her business," I said.

"She talked with you about her business?" he questioned.

"Not her financing books or anything. I asked her in a roundabout way about the confrontation with her business proposal being denied,"

"How in the world did you do that?"

"I'm clever," I laughed.

"I can agree with that," Jasper said.

He pulled partially into the driveway, almost exactly in the same spot from where he had picked me up just a few hours earlier. I waved at the Officers still in their car, keeping an eye on my house while rushing through the snow for warmth. They waved back but didn't try to stop me for conversation, for which I was grateful.

I unlocked the house, entered the warmth, and shed my winter coat, which had clung to me like a second skin. If this weather was truly going to do what the weathermen said it was, we were going to be stuck in the house for a few days. Luckily, I didn't need anything from the stores and would be fine until after the blizzard conditions subsided. The only thing I was going to need saving from was possibly my mind.

I sighed but headed into the living room to read my book again to pass some of the time. I was hardly able to read more than one chapter when my mind wandered off to the subject of Mr. Mysterious.

Getting up, I set my book down and headed into my kitchen, where my window was still not repaired. Now, with the weather putting a damper on things, it would be darker in the dining section for a little while longer. I turned on the lights and stared at my empty table.

I had the sudden idea of using my small dining area as a makeshift location to put together the clues that continued to swarm in my mind. I went to gather papers and sticky notes to make annotations, along with a tablet of paper to piece together all my thoughts so they wouldn't get jumbled.

I started with the basics about the murder of Tom at the Bingo Haven. I put the time that I thought the events happened and would have to see if they matched up later on whenever the storm subsided. I also put the time from the scream and when I found him. I input the information about the forensic accountant and their findings on a separate area and a small sticky note about the testing facility and their employees. There were also the henchmen and their evil plots, and who could their boss be?

Soon, my table was filled with the rantings of a madwoman. There were sticky notes everywhere, and notes from one section to another, but nothing made sense. I looked over at the clock, and it read seven at night. I missed dinner time and would need to find something small to make so I didn't go to bed hungry.

"Jinx, I must have lost track of time," I said out loud.

No mews replied, but I went ahead and filled her kitty dish so she would be able to eat when she felt like it. I rummaged through my freezer, pulled out a distasteful-looking frozen meal, and read the instructions on the back before putting it in the microwave.

I waited for the timer to finish its countdown before pulling out the mushed-together food. It smelled worse than it looked.

Jinx hobbled into the kitchen for her food, but she must have just woken up.

"How nice of you to join me," I laughed.

She continued to mew and purr around my feet as I contemplated throwing away my food. I thought about it for a few seconds, and then, against my inner struggle, I took it toward the cacography of strung-out papers and misconstrued thoughts. I set down the food and began to slowly pick at it before the headache took its toll on me.

It took every ounce in me to finish the food, and with the headache that continued in its wake taking control of all my thoughts, I went to get ready for bed.

I lay in bed, hoping the sudden change would allow my headache to slowly subside. While in bed for a few moments, I quickly learned that my theory was wrong. It seemed that my head resting up on my pillow only made the pounding in my skull worse. I lay there for what seemed like hours until I slowly drifted into sleep.

WHEN I WOKE up a few short hours later, I slowly got out of bed, and it seemed like the headache was back immediately. I contemplated the thought of getting dressed and working back on the project that I started last night.

I decided to try and close my eyes, hoping sleep would retake me, but failed. I finally got out of bed and went to look at what Mother Nature had created with the snow. There was a slight chill in the house, and upon entering the living room, I quickly turned on the TV to the local news channel.

"The temperature has reached sub-zero levels. We advise everyone to stay indoors if you can. Contact your supervisors to see if you must report to work. If any skin is exposed for a short period of time, you will get frostbite. We also ask for you to leave your faucets at a slight trinkle to ensure the pipes don't freeze,"

"Too cold for me out there," I said out loud as I turned the volume down.

I glanced out the window and noticed the Officers were not parked in their usual spot in my driveway. It must be too cold for them to be on patrol. I looked outside through my windows, and what I saw amazed me. The trees that lined the neighborhood were covered in and weighted down with ice.

I stepped away from the window and happened to see my home phone flash with an unheard message.

"Hey, Lola. This is Officer James. We had to pull the security watch from your home due to the weather. We need all able-bodied Officers available for emergencies that might arise due to severe storms that are going to continue to blast our area. I hope you understand, and if you have any questions, feel free to call me at the Station,"

"I'm glad they could be of more use back at the Station and handling real emergencies rather than sitting in the cold in front of the house," I mused.

I deleted the message from the answering machine to free up space in case others needed to get a hold of me but couldn't. I sighed, but the sound of the TV caught my attention even though I had turned it down.

"In other news, we have just received word of a catastrophe that has happened in our town. There was a fire in the warehouse next to the Bingo Haven. Firefighters were unsuccessful in getting to the warehouse in time, and it has unfortunately burned to the ground. The weather has made it more difficult for the first responders to get to the accidents. Which is another reason why we have asked you to remain in the house,"

I sat down, stunned. All of the information that I had just gathered was gone. Literally went up in smoke. I was about to turn off the news when they pulled up the image of the burnt-down building once again.

"We were just informed by one of our sources that there were three injured and one possible fatality,"

The images of the three henchmen came to mind, but it saddened me that there might have been someone severely injured. I didn't want to be saddened by anything else, so I clicked off the TV.

THIRTEEN

It had been four days that I had been cooped up inside my home from the weather. The roads were finally clear and we were dropped from a level three now to a level one. The only thing I could do was watch the news or some other shows that were on or keep working on my project. I tried to do the latter, but my headache would return, causing me to pause in my work.

I talked with Jasper a few times over the phone just to check in to ensure that he hadn't lost power like some of the neighboring areas around us. Luckily, both of us were in the area where the blackouts hadn't occurred. During our talks Jasper had mentioned that a lawyer named Molly Kent had been trying to get a hold of him regarding something about some type of lawsuit that she has been trying to settle. He explained that in the messages that she had left, it was something from an out-of-state case that had been mishandled from years ago. When pressed Jasper wouldn't talk any more about the subject.

I didn't see any point in changing out of my pajamas over the last few days, but since I was going to go investigate the charred remains, I dressed for the cold. I had no appetite this morning, and I wanted to get a head start on checking out the crime scene. I had been watching the news carefully to ensure there were no other fires set within the area. There weren't, which meant there were no pyromaniacs in the area. Which technically was a good thing.

I made sure my outfit was fit for being outside for a period of time and gathered a few supplies, such as a flashlight and anything else that I could think of, before I was about to run out the door.

I had just made my way over to the front door when there was a sudden knock, which startled me. I opened it carefully, not sure who could be on the other side.

"Can I help you?" I asked the younger woman.

"Hello, my name is Molly Kent, and I'm a lawyer," she began.

"Is there something I can help you with, Ms. Kent?"

"I've been trying to get a hold of a man named Jasper, and my sources have told me that the two of you are really close friends,"

"I see. Well, as you can see, he is not here at the moment,"

"Oh, I know where he is. I actually came by to talk with you about a few things,"

"Me?"

"Yes. How much do you really know about Jasper's past?"

"I know enough about my friend, and I'm sure that whatever I don't know, he will tell me when he is ready. I'm sorry to be rude, but I was just heading out the door,"

"Maybe we could talk over a nice cup of coffee or maybe a small bite to eat?" she asked eagerly.

"Maybe some other time. Like I said, I was heading out the door before you stopped by,"

"Oh," she said sadly.

She handed me her business card and walked away toward a shiny new black car. I waited a few heartbeats before I headed to my own vehicle to start it up, hoping that the cold hadn't messed up the battery.

The engine roared to life, and I pulled out of my driveway without any issues. I turned the heat on, hoping it would warm up quickly, and drove around town looking at the destruction that had happened to our area. There were still downed power lines and fallen trees in several spots, but there was also a good part of the town that hadn't been touched. Luckily, the area of town that the Bingo Haven was in the area that must have been in Mother Nature's good graces.

I parked my car in the same old parking lot, and the business hadn't changed since the murder. People were still coming through the doors at an odd pace. I was usually one of those patrons, just going through the motions of another day. Not today, though, I had a mission, and I wasn't going to be deterred.

I didn't wait for an invite; I walked away from Bingo Haven's inviting doors and went straight for the burned-down warehouse. Honestly, the Bingo Haven was lucky that it hadn't caught fire, too, since the buildings were practically joined together.

The image from the news didn't do the scene any justice because it was actually worse in person. I trudged through the burnt-down debris that was left and found a spot that was oddly colored and had the impression of a human silhouette. I would have had to guess that this was where the remains were found after the incident.

I took a step back, and the reality of not being here forever hit me like a ton of bricks. Looking at the remnants of a life was world-shattering and made me almost crumple on the spot. *Not now.*

I walked away from the area and tried to rummage through anything that the fire might not have destroyed.

"Lola?" Officer James called out.

I was startled and stopped what I was doing.

"Officer James?" I questioned.

"What are you doing here? This is an active investigation for the arson unit. You shouldn't be poking around. There might be something dangerous lurking,"

"Fine. I'll go, but you should know that I was poking around here before the building burnt down, and there was some shady stuff going on,"

"Care to elaborate? I'm sure you were invited into the building?" Officer James laughed.

"Like you guys say on the news all the time about open investigations. No comment,"

Officer James walked forward and helped me around the debris that was still scattered across the area.

"Thank you, by the way. Was there a fatality like the news said?" I asked.

"I hate to say it, but yes. I'm not at liberty to discuss the open case, nor do I think that the family would want me to say anything..." he trailed off.

"I understand. It's just sad to think that there were human remains just a few feet away from where we're standing. It kind of puts things into perspective,"

"By the way, has a lawyer by the name of Molly Kent been trying to get in touch with you?" he asked.

"As a matter of fact, she stopped by my house right before I left and wanted to know some information about Jasper's past. Do you know anything about it?"

"I try to not make it a habit to research every person in the area," he chuckled.

"It was worth a shot," I said as I began to walk back to my car.

"If it's bothering you, why not ask him about it? As long as I've known the two of you, both of you have been thick as thieves. I'm sure he can clear up whatever it is making you uncomfortable,"

"I think you're right. I might wait for him to finish his shift today and just ask him about it,"

"Is he supposed to be working?"

"As far as I know he is,"

"Maybe he caught a ride with a friend? I don't see his truck parked anywhere?"

"Strange, maybe he called in for the day. I'll swing by his place and check on him,"

"Take it easy, Lola, just let me know if you need anything,"

"Quick question, have there been any updates on the case of Tom?"

"I can't discuss anything with you here, but if you want, call the station to see when Franks and I will both be in, and we can go over anything you'd like. I don't want to discuss anything pertinent outside of the Station walls," he said, looking around as though someone was listening.

His uneasiness made me suspicious, but what was I going to do? Question him here in the parking lot? I had this unnerving feeling that Jasper was hiding something, and him not showing up for his usual shift at his favorite place was more than enough reason to check on him.

"I'll see when I can maybe make it over to the Station; it might not be today, though," I said as I waved my goodbye.

"I'll see you around then,"

Climbing back into my car, I rushed through the mundane motions of driving back to the complex. Instead of turning onto my street, I turned on the one before, which would take me to Jasper's.

I pulled into the driveway, and there was his truck. I quickly got out, and I placed my hand on the hood to check to see if there was any warmth, as though he had been somewhere. It was cold.

I walked to the door, and Jasper was already there waiting to greet me, but this time, there was no warmth to his welcome.

"Hello, Lola,"

"Jasper?"

"Would you like to come in?"

I stepped into his usual, well-organized home, which was now disheveled as though someone had broken in.

"What happened?"

He stepped away from the door and walked into the living room, and that was when I noticed the bottle of liquor in his hand. He tipped it up and took a big swig before picking something off a shelf and throwing it at a wall.

"Nothing," he muttered.

"I don't know what this is, but it sure isn't nothing,"

"DON'T YOU SEE! THEY FOUND ME!" he shouted.

"What are you talking about?"

I walked through his house, which was almost the same layout as my own, and started a pot of coffee to try and sober him up.

"My past has finally caught up to me," he thundered.

"What past?" I asked, walking back into the living room.

"There is quite a bit you don't know about me," he began as I sat on the couch across from him. "I was once in a thriving cult as an accountant,"

I didn't say anything and waited for him to continue.

"At first, I didn't know that it was a cult per se. I had heard of the rumors, but I didn't believe them. I had been a freelance accountant, and I just wanted my own permanent place to work. It had been rough for so long that I was willing to take the easy way out. When I went to the residence for an open interview, they were thrilled to find someone so diverse and willing to work with new clients. We agreed upon a set salary, and I got to work immediately," he said as he slouched farther into the chair.

"Go on,"

"Lola, their booking system was a mess. There were so many discrepancies that I thought I was going to go bald at a young age from the stress. After almost a year of going through the entire system and finally figuring out what happened to their money, they invited me to stay full-time. Of course, I agreed because I was the one who found that others had stolen from the organization and had the proof that was needed to convict the thieves. I also didn't want anyone else to jump in and screw anything up that I had finally been able to fix," he paused. "Are you following all of this?"

"I'm trying to. Let me get this straight, you were part of some kind of cult?" I questioned.

"They soon called me one of their own, and I'll admit that it was odd at first, but it was a tight-knit community of sorts. After a few months, I started to attend their meetings and do other things. Before I knew it, I began to share some of their beliefs..." he trailed off.

"So you became a full believer in your employer's ways?" I asked as he took another swig.

He set the bottle down and ran his hand over his face as though he were embarrassed.

"Yes,"

"Do you have those beliefs now?"

"No. After a few years of working for them, some of our members suddenly began to disappear. I started to become inquisitive. The more I dug into the cult, the more I was able to uncover their dirty secrets,"

"Which were?"

"I'm not at liberty to discuss. I signed a form that forbids me to discuss the case's details without a lawyer,"

"The lawyer that has been coming around, Molly Kent, is she the lawyer that you worked with?"

"No. I worked with the FBI's lawyers to ensure there would be an air-tight case against the cultist. Molly Kent was one of their lawyers. There were threats against my life, and I was placed into protective custody for over a year. In and out of safe houses and cheap take-out and the constant active threat that the cultist continued to send for me,"

"Are you in witness protection?"

"No, although that was a possible option, but the threat subsided, and after the court dates, I was finally able to walk away a free man,"

"So, if you're not in the witness protection program..."

"Like I said, I walked away a free man who needed a new start. I left everything from the apartment that I had when I lived on the compound site and needed a fresh start. The FBI gave me enough money for a full tank of gas for my truck, and I never looked back. I moved five states over and thought about changing my name, but I couldn't bring myself to do it at the end of the day. Luckily I was able to save a little money for hotel rooms here and there and eventually some crappy apartments until I was able to get on my feet,"

"So what is Molly Kent doing here now?"

"Isn't that the million-dollar question,"

Jasper hoisted himself up and began to pace around the small living room area. I was able to smell the coffee, and I managed to walk around him to make a cup for him and myself. Maybe it would help settle his nerves.

When I walked back into the living room, Jasper sat back down and stared out the window with a dazed look. I walked over with his cup and made sure he had a full grasp on it before releasing it.

"What do you think Molly wants?" I asked.

"I'm not sure," he said while taking a sip from his cup.

I was about to sit back down with my cup to continue to console my friend when there was a sudden knock on the door.

"Don't answer it," he said, hands shaking, spilling his coffee.

"We don't even know if it's her. Also, if it is, then we can figure out what it is that she wants from you," I countered.

I walked away from him and went to answer the door.

"Please! Don't!" he shouted.

It was already too late. I opened the door, and to nobody's surprise, it was Molly Kent with a broad smile.

"Nice to see you, Lola. May I come in?"

"I'm sorry, my friend is not up for any additional visitors at the moment, but I will personally make sure that when he is feeling up to it, that he gets in contact with you,"

"Ah, dodging me again, I see,"

"I'm sorry?"

"I've been looking for him for a long time, and then, low and behold, his name shows up again from a source telling me that he had settled down in a smaller town and retired from his old accounting lifestyle. Tell Jasper that I will talk with him sooner or later," Molly said before turning on her heel to leave.

FOURTEEN

"You're going to have to talk with her at some point,"

"No, I don't,"

"You can't ignore her forever. Do you have any way to contact the FBI agents who handled the case with you?"

"Somewhere tucked away in my safe,"

"The key that was in the safe at the Bingo Haven had the cultist symbol on it, right?"

"Yes,"

"What if this whole money laundering scheme is also based from the cultists?"

"Are you crazy? How would that even be possible?"

"From the little bit you just told me, it sounds like they had quite the influential reach. What's to say that the person who is behind this entire scheme wasn't coordinated from the cult."

"I helped disband the entire organization," Jasper countered.

"Their lawyer found you, so it must be up and running again. Or at least, something is happening within the organization,"

"This can't be happening," Jasper said as he began to hyperventilate.

"Calm down, and we can figure this out together,"

"I think it would be for the better if you left," he said with a shaky breath.

"You want me to leave you alone so you can try to figure this out on your own?" I countered.

"I'm not sure what I'm going to do, but I think I would prefer to be alone at the moment,"

"Well, Jasper, if that is how you feel, I won't overstay my welcome. Please call me if you need help with anything,"

I walked out of his house, not knowing if my friend was truly going to be alright. He had never been curt with me before, but I could tell that this was something from his past that he truly wanted to keep hidden. I hated that I was going to have to bring this up again since the note attached to the key was the same symbol from the cultist from his past.

As I walked to my car, I didn't dare look to the ground; I didn't want Jasper, whom I knew was watching from the windows, to think that I was distraught.

There was a prickling sensation on my skin, and I looked around and found Molly sitting in her car with a camera sticking out of the window aimed at Jasper's house. She wasn't going to give up after a simple brush-off.

I walked toward her, and she was about to put the car into gear.

"Wait!" I called out.

This stopped her in her tracks, and she didn't pull away even though she had been caught red-handed.

"We should talk," I said, coming closer to the car.

"I mean, you did catch me taking surveillance of Jasper's house, so why not? When?"

"Now," I countered.

"Are you a local?"

"Of course, I can tell that you're not. Why don't you follow me to a place that is cozy and will offer us privacy as well,"

"Alright, sounds like a deal,"

I rushed back to my car and quickly got ready for the short drive over to a wonderful cafe that only served breakfast and lunch. While driving down the side streets, I made sure Molly wouldn't get lost along the way; I just hoped that she wouldn't change her mind about our meeting.

We soon pulled into the parking lot, and it looked like most of the afternoon crowd had already eaten. We both exited our vehicles, and I waited for her to gather her paperwork.

"Cozy?" Molly said as she walked closer to the entrance.

"It doesn't look like much, but the food here is wonderful,"

As we walked inside, I could see her clutching her paperwork as though it was part of her lifeline.

"Nobody is going to bite, y'know," I laughed as we walked toward an empty table.

She set the paperwork down, then her purse, all the while glancing around the area as though she were searching for danger.

"I'll admit, I'm not used to the smaller town generosity," she said.

"I'll agree. We are a smaller town compared to the larger cities, but we are by far not considered that small," I laughed.

"How does this restaurant work? I've never been to one where you just seat yourself,"

"A server will be over shortly to take our order just like any other place,"

"There are usually lines out of the door just waiting for a place to sit for lunch during the week,"

"That doesn't sound like a very happy place to be," I mused.

"I'll admit, this town has had several perks, and I would rather stay in a place like this,"

The server walked over, stopping our conversation. We both ordered drinks and food and then waited for more privacy.

"I believe we need to have a serious conversation about why you want to speak with Jasper so desperately,"

"Well, I can't completely tell you because of attorney-client privilege,"

"So this has something to do with the cultist that Jasper helped put away years ago..."

"Nobody is supposed to know about it. How do you?"

"I asked Jasper, and that was all he was willing to tell me,"

"My client wants to speak with Jasper about some details from the past case,"

"Just talk?"

"Yes,"

The waitress returned with our food, and both of us began to eat slowly and continue our conversation.

"If I'm going to try to convince him to meet with you, I'm going to need a little bit more information,"

"All I can say is there is a new leader of the activist group, and they had some questions about the past. Unfortunately, I don't know the questions because the leader would like to speak with him personally. I assured him that I could have Jasper located and then just video conference him, but that wasn't good enough. I also tried to have him write the questions down, but again, he wasn't happy with that suggestion,"

"What's this new leader like?"

"I can't give out his name, but many have called him Mr. Mysterious,"

"Really?" I couldn't help but giggle a little at the name.

"What's so funny?" she asked with a smile.

"It's just that name has been used more than once over these last few days. There's no way they could be the same man?" I chuckled in between bites.

"I'm going to say no. My client travels often for his line of business and often finds himself in odd situations. Sometimes he does frequent Bingo halls, though,"

"You don't say," I said, mulling over the information.

"I've never had food made with such detail. I mean, yeah, in other states, it does have fancier food plated a little differently, but the portions here are so much larger. Not to mention, the taste is phenomenal. I could convince myself to stay here just on the food alone,"

"Why don't we order some dessert?"

We mulled over the menu for a moment and then placed our order once again. Before we could continue our conversation, she quickly appeared with our pies.

"That's it! I'm officially staying in town," she said excitedly with a mouth full of food.

"When it comes to Jasper, I'm not sure if I will be able to get him to sit down with you. I will talk with him, but he is pretty set on not being around you. Were you the lawyer on the original case?"

"Thank you for being honest with me, and yes. It was one of the first cases that made my career. Even though my client didn't win, it opened a few doors for a wide array of new clientele,"

"Have you been busy this entire time with the same client? I mean, I thought Jasper had put the original activist away in prison. How did the group get started again?"

"That is an interesting story. How about this? If you can convince Jasper to speak with me, then I'll tell you both the story,"

"Seems like you drive a hard bargain. I'll talk with my friend. When do you want to meet again?"

She thought for a moment before writing something on the back of a business card.

"Here is my card with my cell number on it. Call me when he is ready,"

The small restaurant that we had been sitting in was starting to close for the day. Molly placed some money on the table for our meal before clutching the papers she had originally carried in.

"Thank you!" I called after her.

The waitress came over, and I made sure the money that was left behind would cover our meal along with a tip. I didn't want to leave, knowing that we might have shorted the restaurant.

I walked back outside into the cold and called Jasper from my cell phone. I wasn't too surprised when he didn't answer. I didn't want to crowd him so I decided to head home instead. I had spent most of the day out and about and just wanted to relax.

Driving back to the neighborhood always brought a smile and a certain warmth deep within me. I always thought our smallish town was safe, but the most recent happenings made me rethink my past assumptions.

Just in the last few weeks, there had been two murders; I was going to need to go to my chaos board to check a few details. Also, I would need to do a few internet searches to come up with some information from the cult of which Jasper was once a part of.

Once inside, the urge to find out more information about the owner of the Bingo Haven and the cult was driving me crazy. I did a quick pass by the phone and noticed there was an unlistened message.

"Hey, Lola, this is Alan. I know you wanted me to fix the window, but I'm not sure if I'll be able to complete the job. Y'know, for my own safety and all. I hope you're not mad at me. Please give me a callback,"

I couldn't blame him; after all, he was sent off to the hospital via paramedic the last time he was here. I was going to need to find someone once winter was over. I picked up the phone and dialed his return number.

"Hello?"

"Alan? This is Lola,"

"Oh, hi. I'm sorry for just leaving a message like that, but I talked it over with my wife, and she is really concerned for me to return to the job site. I know I started on the work, but to put her mind at ease along with my own, I'm going to have to drop the work," he said sadly.

"I understand. I don't want you or your wife to worry just for a job. Do you have anybody in mind, maybe for after winter?"

"I might. Let me give them a call, and if they are interested, I'll give them your information. Does that sound ok?"

"It sounds wonderful. Thank you again for what you were able to complete, and I hope you don't have any ill feelings toward an older lady,"

"I never blamed you for the accident,"

"I'll talk to you later,"

"Bye, Lola,"

I set the phone back on the receiver and headed toward my still lightless dining area. There, on the table and partial wall space, was what looked like a full conspiracy board. There was the first murder from the Bingo Haven, now the second death right beside it. There were a few suspects that I had in mind. There were the three goons from the restaurant, then Mr. Mysterious was also in the mix. Who was this new player from the cultist? What was Molly's involvement?

I hadn't even started my research project, and the headache was coming back. I wondered how detectives were able to do this on a regular basis. I took a few over-the-counter headache pills and pulled out a pen and paper to start my research project on my phone.

At first, I looked up the owner of the Bingo Haven, but the only information I was able to pull was the manager, Ruby. There were some articles hinting about the possibility of an owner, but no picture or information.

I opened a new tab on my phone and began to look for major cult crimes that would have included an accountant. There were a few vague articles, but I didn't see anything concrete.

Feeling defeated, I turned off my phone, and my headache got worse. The only thing to do was turn away from the project and allow my inner brain cells to rest and relax.

I made some tea on the stove and went to unwind in my chair for a few moments. My cell phone began to ring, and Jasper's name lit up on the screen.

"Hello?" I answered.

"Hey, Lola. I've been doing some thinking all day. I couldn't help but see you talking with that lawyer, Molly?"

"I was going to talk to you about it in a few days once you've had time to think some things through. Since you called, I'll go ahead and tell you now. I had lunch with Molly and asked her about what she wanted to speak with you about,"

"What did she say?"

"Her client wants to speak with you about some things from the past,"

"Did she go into detail?"

"No, but I did tell her that I would speak with you about meeting with her,"

"I'll think about it," he said before hanging up.

The tea kettle began to whistle from the kitchen, alerting me that the water was ready.

FIFTEEN

A few more days had passed, and not another word from Jasper. It was odd that he never called back or bothered to stop by for some company. Maybe this was a bigger deal than I originally thought.

I never called the Police Station to see when both James and Franks would be available. I wanted more than anything for this case to just hurry up so I could go back to my boring, mundane life.

I guess now that the weather had stopped trying to freeze us to death, it was as good as any to try and get some more answers. I went to the house phone, and my hand hovered slightly over it as though it had a mind of its own. I had to force myself to pick it up and dial the number to the main Station.

"Hello, this is the Greenfield Police Station. How may I direct your call?" a female voice asked.

"I need to speak with Officer James, please,"

"I'm not sure if he is in at the moment, but I'll transfer. Please hold,"

There was the average elevator music that played for a brief moment before the line picked up.

"Hello, this is Officer James,"

"This is Lola. I was wondering when would be a good time for me to swing by and maybe look over some things from the case?"

"Lola, I was starting to wonder if you had given up on us. You can come over now if you'd like,"

"Alright, I'll see you shortly,"

I hung up and quickly went to gather my purse before heading out the door. It was still cold thus ensuring a coat was still needed on this bright and sunny day. Thanks to no windchill, it was going to be a beautiful day, no doubt tricking us into thinking that spring was right around the corner. I had lived in the area for too many years and knew better.

I made quick work through the morning traffic and pulled into the parking lot, finding a spot not too far to walk. I glanced around, and if you didn't know the city's secrets, it would have been beautiful.

Upon entering the Station's front doors, I saw paper snowflakes hanging from the ceiling. It brought a smile to my face and a fond memory of when I worked at the library; we would always have the kids make us some for winter decorations.

I walked past the receptionist and headed straight for Officer James and Franks' desks. When I found them, they were both laughing and drinking their coffee at a leisurely pace. They were staring at their corkboard, which looked a lot more organized than my table of misconstrued thoughts.

"So, you weren't kidding when you said I could stop by,"

"Lola! About time you made it," Officer James said, almost spilling his coffee onto his uniform.

"Easy there, I don't think there are any hot leads to follow up with. No need to dump your coffee," I laughed.

"She's right, y'know. We don't have anything really concrete to go on," Officer Franks added.

"Why, Franks, I've never known you to be so lapsed in your pursuit of justice," Officer James said.

"It's getting closer and closer to Christmas," he added.

"Is it really?" I asked, shocked.

"Yeah, haven't you been paying attention to the calendar?" Officer Franks asked.

"Actually, I haven't been. I've been so preoccupied by the case I haven't been able to focus on much else," I added sadly.

"What have you been able to uncover on your own?" Officer James asked, leaning back in his office chair, which creaked from under his weight.

I went closer to look at their board, and there wasn't anything that I hadn't already solved on my own.

"Can you look into something and be discreet?" I asked.

"Like what?" Officer Franks mused.

"A case that is out of state. Even FBI territory," I inquired.

"Why would we want to check in on something from another agency?" Officer James questioned.

"I have a hunch, and I need more information," I said meekly.

"If the agents on the case call us from poking around, I'm going to completely blame it on you," Officer James joked.

"I'll take it all; if my hunch is correct, then I might know who killed Tom and solve his case," I added.

"So, what does he need to look for exactly?" Officer Franks added.

"It involves a case about Jasper and an out-of-state incident,"

"What?" Officer James asked.

"I have some of the details, but Jasper wouldn't go into too much. In fact, he told me to leave once he was done telling me about it and also proceeded to hang up on me after we spoke on the phone regarding a lawyer from his past,"

"To think you know everything about everyone," Officer Franks said.

"I didn't even know about it until the lawyer Molly Kent came around asking questions,"

"I can work with that information about Jasper, and the name of the lawyer helps, too," Officer James said as he began to type into his computer.

"How big was this case?" Officer James asked.

"Why not finding it?" Officer Franks joked.

"Actually, that's the opposite of what's happening. There is a giant case involving multiple suspects, and according to the case reports, it was a cult group claimed to be activist?" Officer James added with a hint of surprise.

"Yeah, that would be the case. Do you have access to everything, or how does this work?" I asked.

"What information are you looking for exactly?" Officer Franks asked.

"I need to know who went to prison because of Jasper's testimony," I said in a low voice.

Officer James clicked some buttons on the computer and began to do some deep diving into the information that was before him. I wanted to skim over his shoulder but thought it would be rude. I'm not privy to the information that is listed in the database.

"I see that Roger DeLuca was in charge of the activist group. He and several others were put away for a long time without the chance of parole. I see murder was one of the charges, and conspiracy to commit murder was also added to later charges," Officer James read aloud.

"Can you tell me who the attempted murder charges were from?" I asked softly.

"Let me guess, Jasper?" Officer Franks guessed.

"Yeah, it also said that DeLuca had an up-and-coming protege, who went by the name of Mr. Mysterious in the group. No real names were added as part of a plea bargain, and this guy never served time,"

If I could have seen a mirror, I would have sworn that my face would have mimicked a deer in the headlights.

"Is there a picture of the guy who struck the plea bargain?" Officer Franks asked.

"Let me look around the file a little more," Officer James said, studying the case more closely.

I was on pins and needles, waiting for the answer.

"Anytime now," Officer Franks joked.

"No, there is no picture of him," Officer James added.

I released the breath that I had been apparently holding. We would never catch a break on this case. Although, my suspicions were getting clearer the more I thought about it. Mr. Mysterious had to be the same one that was the owner of the Bingo Hall.

"What are you thinking, Lola?" Officer James asked.

"If I tell you, I might sound crazy," I laughed nervously.

"It's got to be better than anything we were able to come up with," Officer Franks said, getting up from his chair to look at the corkboard.

"Mind if I sit down? This is going to sound crazy," I asked.

"Go right ahead," Officer Franks pointed to his chair, which he had just vacated.

I began to tell them about everything that had happened and all that I knew, including the meeting with Molly and how the new owner wanted to meet with Jasper.

"You weren't kidding; that is one giant tale from start to finish," Officer James said.

"Although, what you said does make sense in a way. I'm not sure why he would need to launder the money through the Bingo Hall?" Officer Franks asked.

"Well, before, it seemed like the cult was able to use Jasper as the fall guy and move the money whenever they needed. Since Molly is asking for Jasper, her client won't allow her to ask questions on his behalf. It would be safe to assume that Jasper isn't safe wherever he goes. My guess would be that the client wants some information from Jasper, but I'm not sure what?" I said.

"What if he wants to hire Jasper? Y'know, to work for him again or his cult group again?" Officer Franks asked.

"Jasper would never go for it. What if Jasper helped hide the money from the group? Where did the funds and the rest of the group that wasn't caught up in the scandal go?" Officer James asked.

"How sure are you of your theory?" Officer Franks asked.

"It's the only thing that makes sense. There are too many unanswered questions, and the only thing I can comprehend would be this Mr. Mysterious guy everybody talked about,"

"What about business records? There has to be a record of whoever opened the business or at least put in the request. Their name and ID have to be on file with the courts," Officer James said, turning back to the computer and typing in more information at a rate that I would never be able to match.

"Wouldn't a smart man use a decoy or somebody from within the cult to put up his or her information so if anything ever happened, it would fall to them?" I asked.

"He has to make a mistake somewhere, right?" Officer Franks added.

"Let's see what the computer has to say about the businesses,"

"It looks like an IT guy from a company that I've never heard of before," Officer James said.

"Look up the owner of the warehouse next to the Bingo Hall," I said.

Officer James again went to the computer and then put his hand up as if in defeat.

"What?" Officer Franks asked.

"It's the same guy who owns the Bingo Haven," Officer James pointed at the screen.

"Last question. Look up to see if this guy has any connection to Vixen's Bingo Palace and Victoria," I asked.

"From what I can quickly glance through, they used to date in the past," Officer James added while sitting back in his chair.

"So, not only was Victoria a part of the cultist past, she also knows the supposed owner. She might be the key to solving the entire case," I said, trying to work through the process.

Officer James got up from his seat in a rush and left the area where we had been conversing.

"What just happened?" I asked.

"Sometimes he gets what I call a gut feeling. He will just get up and run away, and usually, I have to follow and try to figure out what he already did. Thanks for stopping by, Lola; you might have solved the case. Let us do some more digging and see what we can find out,"

"It was my pleasure. I'm glad that I could help, even if it was just a little,"

I got up and Officer Franks made sure that I made it out of the building before what I would have guessed was to follow his partner. I left the Station and pondered on what we discussed. I made the quick decision to head over to Vixen's Bingo Palace to talk with Victoria again.

I wasted no time with pleasantries toward the staff and made my way to the raised voices that were coming from an empty room. It sounded like Jasper and Victoria were arguing.

I had made my way to the closed room when suddenly the voices stopped, and the door opened.

"Lola?" Jasper croaked.

"Surprised?" I asked.

"This isn't what it looks like," he pleaded.

"Lola?" Victoria asked, shocked.

"I know," I said.

Jasper didn't say anything, but his face paled at my simple accusation.

"I'm sorry?" Victoria snapped.

"You know who Mr. Mysterious is. You've known this entire time, and you've been trying to connect the dots back to him. The real question is, why?" I asked.

"Well..." Victoria stuttered.

"My guess is you wanted the Bingo Haven and Vixen's Bingo Palace to be one operation. This way, you could oversee what exactly was going on behind the scenes. Also, see the flow of money coming and going. You want to take over the cult," I implied.

"Where did you get all of this information?" Victoria snapped again.

"That's a great question, and I'm not going to answer. Jasper, you have a lot of explaining to do," I said before I walked away from the pair.

"SECURITY!" Victoria shouted.

"Don't bother, we'll see ourselves out," Jasper shouted.

I continued my way out of the establishment with Jasper hot on my trail.

"Lola, wait!" he shouted.

I didn't stop until we were well away from the security of the building, and nobody could eavesdrop on our conversation.

"Were you going to tell me?" I asked.

"Lola, like you said. We're not dating, so I don't have to tell you what I do," Jasper countered.

"I don't mean that. Someone tried to murder you in the past. I went down to the Station and spoke with Officers Franks and James, and we came up with quite the theory," I paused. "Care to guess what we were able to put together?" I said, pointing a finger at him.

"I, uh,"

"Exactly. The only reason why I was so fixated on meeting with Molly was to see what she wanted. Personally, I think she is a nice person. Professionally, I find her business a little skeptical,"

"I'm not going to meet with her,"

"After what I gathered from the Officers, you might be in danger,"

"From who?"

"I think you know more than you're letting on,"

"Let's just agree to disagree," he muttered before heading to his truck.

I watched him drive away with tires squealing on the pavement as he sped away from here. I couldn't help but wonder if he was trying to get away from Victoria and the cult, or was it me?

My cell phone began to ring in my purse, and I fished it out. I checked the caller ID, and I didn't recognize it, but I answered it nonetheless.

"Hello?"

"Lola? Hi, this is Molly. Were you able to speak with Jasper about meeting my client?" she asked.

"I've been able to talk with him, but he doesn't feel up to it," I answered.

"Oh, too bad. I'll just keep trying. My client is pretty insistent on getting a meeting with him. Can you just let him know that I'm not going to go away? One way or another, there will be a meeting,"

"I'll be sure to pass along the message,"

I hung up the phone and leaned against my car, pondering what to do next.

SIXTEEN

After the confrontation that Jasper and I just had I didn't really want to talk with him so soon. I was stuck between wanting to help my friend and being mad at him. My inner friend won and decided to text him before entering my car and began to head toward the direction of home.

As soon as I entered my car, I changed my mind about going home and headed toward my old stomping grounds. The place where I had spent so many hours helping others, making crafts with kids, and countless other things.

Pulling into the parking lot, I couldn't help but to go to my usual parking spot. I got out, and the memories came flooding back. *Why did I retire? To play Bingo?*

There was an ache in my chest even though there had only been a few months of work separation. *Maybe I would come back part-time? Maybe a volunteer?*

I walked through the front door, and the smell of home hit me. At that moment, I realized why Jasper still worked, even part-time. Days have become a blur, and seeing all of the Christmas decorations brought a joyous feeling to my cold heart. I hadn't really thought about the holidays and what they meant to everyone here in town.

"Ms. Lola!" a child shouted.

"Thomas! It's so good to see you," I said as the small boy ran into my arms for a big hug.

"Have you come back to work in the library again? I sure have missed you," he said, wiping his hands on his pants.

"I haven't decided yet,"

"Mrs. Lovely, it's so nice to see you," I said to his mother.

"Lola, I'm so glad that you stopped by today. You know Thomas hasn't really been the same since you left story time. Change is hard on him and others like him," she said.

"There's nothing wrong with him. Autism or not, your child is just fine," I chided her.

"I'm glad Thomas was able to see you today. It will make him more delightful for a few days," Mrs. Lovely said.

Thinking on her words, I walked away from them and headed deeper into the labyrinth of books, which were still nice and tidy on their shelves. There were new books always being added throughout the seasons, and I was able to see several of them displayed on a table in the middle of the room.

"Lola? It's so good to see you. How have you been since the retirement party?" Brittany asked.

"Lately, I've been busy,"

"With the murder of Tom?" Brittany asked.

"Yeah, I forgot how fast local gossip travels in this town," I laughed slightly.

"It must have been awful to watch him be murdered,"

"Well, I didn't actually see him go down. I just heard the scream of the server who found him and saw the body on the ground,"

"Rumor has it that there was the sound of gunshots that echoed through the entire hall,"

"No, there weren't any sounds of gunshots. In fact, I didn't see the weapon at all. The killer must have taken it with them," I said, only half paying attention to the conversation.

"Oh, well, there are some people waiting to check out some books. It was nice to see you, Lola,"

"You too, Brittany,"

I checked my phone to see if there had been any word from Jasper, but he didn't respond. There was just a note stating that he had read the message and what time he read it. At least he looked at it and I had done my part.

I stuck around the library to see if there would be any other dirt I could find out from the locals who were not so willing to speak with me. A few long and agonizing hours had passed, and nothing was ever mentioned. I was beginning to wonder if my super sleuth powers were starting to wear off.

"Hello, Victoria!" Brittany's voice called from her desk.

"Hello, Brittany. Has my usual business partner made it in yet?" Victoria asked.

"No, not yet," Brittany responded.

"Ok. Just let him know that I'm over by the computers if he doesn't see me,"

Business partner?

"Hello, are you Victoria Smith? The owner of Vixen's Bingo Hall?" a male voice asked.

I wished I could see the pair, but I didn't want to give away my secret hiding place and get caught eavesdropping.

"I am. Who are you?" Victoria asked.

"My name is Alex, and I work for the paper. I've gotten a lead on a story that I can't seem to shake. I've come to get the insider information, and one of my sources says that you were the one I needed to talk with," Alex said.

"Who is your source?" Victoria asked.

"I'm not at liberty to say,"

"I don't have to speak with you about anything. Your source is wrong," she argued.

"My sources never lie. Once I'm done interviewing you, I'll be on my way to look for Lola. Her previous place of employment was here at the library?" he asked.

"Yes, she worked here for many years. Now she favors Bingo Haven with her friend Jasper,"

"Jasper, you say?"

I tried to inch closer to get a better look at this Alex person. I was going to have to ask around and see if he was really telling the truth about working for the local paper. I saw him jotting down several notes in a small journal.

"What other kind of notes do you have locked away?"

"Oh, nothing. These are just my thoughts and sub-clue contexts that I constantly refer to when I am out chasing leads," he chuckled.

"Are you working on the Tom Burchfield case?"

"That and a few others. Do you know where I could find Lola at this time? According to her DMV records, her car is parked in the parking lot, but I haven't seen her,"

"You have DMV records?" Victoria asked with mock surprise.

"You don't?"

Great. Now, I really needed to figure out who his sources might be. I didn't think DMV records were public knowledge.

"That's privileged information," Victoria said haughtily.

"Again, I did say that I had sources. You never know who it might be," Alex replied.

"If you're still looking for Lola, I haven't seen her since I've been here. She might be in a back room or something. You're welcome to look around if the librarians let you, which is doubtful. I'm here waiting..."

"To meet with your business associate?" Alex said, finishing her sentence.

She scowled at him but didn't say anything else. She opened her mouth to say something else when Alex cut her off.

"Sources, remember? I'll be heading on my way to see if I can locate some other people and finally put their names to their faces,"

I couldn't see his face, but I saw that he was a taller man with a brutish figure. I wondered if he just intimidated his sources into giving him information. He was heading out the door when he suddenly turned back to say one last thing to Victoria.

"Oh, I don't think that business partner of yours will be meeting you today," he said ominously.

"What?"

He didn't say anything else; he just left the library and Victoria to stew on his last words. How would he know that her business partner wasn't going to make it?

Victoria got up from her seat, which caused it to scrape against the floor, making a loud noise before she exited the building.

"You can come out of hiding now, Lola," Brittany said a little loudly.

I walked out of my space with a smirk because she had known I was there all along.

"It's my job to ensure everybody has been helped within the library. That includes the coming and going of patrons," she added.

"Have you ever seen that man before? Alex?" I asked her.

"No, but that doesn't always mean anything,"

"Your right, I just have this feeling that something is off about him,"

"I have someone close to me who works for the paper. Do you want me to ask around and get back with you about his employment?" Brittany asked.

"Don't cause any trouble, but that would be amazing,"

"Anything for an old friend,"

I went to leave the library and waited in the foyer to check out in the parking lot to see if anybody would be waiting by my car. There wasn't, which must mean the coast was clear.

Before I was able to make it outside, I heard Brittany's voice talking on the phone to someone she must know at the paper. I just hoped that she wasn't going to be stirring up trouble.

I rushed to my car not waiting for anybody that might be lurking within their own vehicles.

"Lola!" Brittany shouted.

She rushed to my car and shivered in the cold due to not wearing any proper winter gear.

"What is it?" I asked, trying to hurry her up.

"My guy says there hasn't been any new hire at the local paper. He's the head editor, and he's the one who assigns the cases to each reporter. That means he's a phony, and you need to be careful," she said before running back into the warmth of the building.

I knew something felt off.

If this Alex person was supposed to be a reporter and his sources were able to give him so much information, who was he really working for? Was he a private investigator looking to help solve Tom Burchfield's case?

That conclusion didn't feel right. What if he worked for Mr. Mysterious and was trying to locate us for his own personal reasons.

That made more sense. Greenfield is a smaller town, too small for a P.I. to be lurking around in the shadows.

The few hours that I had spent out and about today had caused a major hunger to fill within me, and instead of heading home to another frozen dinner, I decided to head over to a local pasta place.

It was right before their dinner rush, and apparently, today was Friday, as that was what their menu advertised for their daily special. I didn't want the fish and settled for shrimp alfredo with a salad.

My usual waitress came over and took my order, and I looked around at the other patrons within the establishment. I couldn't believe my eyes. There sat Alex at a table all by himself. He was going over paperwork when he suddenly looked up, and our eyes locked. He smiled sinisterly in my direction.

He got up from his seat, gathered his papers, and headed in my direction. A feeling of dread came over me, but I knew that I was going to have to confront him.

"Lola, is it?" he asked.

"Yes? You are?" I asked, pretending not to know.

"Let me introduce myself. My name is Alex, and I work for the paper, and I'm trying to solve Tom Burchfield's murder,"

"Nice to meet you,"

"Do you mind if I sit down?"

I motioned with my hand for him to sit, and he did, setting his papers down next to him in the booth. He waved his server down and explained in a matter-of-fact tone that he would be eating with his friend and asked to have the food moved to my table.

"To what do I owe this visit?" I asked.

"Well," he began, but paused when my waitress brought out our salads. "Like I said, I'm trying to get the scoop on what happened at the Bingo Haven on the day of the murder,"

"I see. Did you get the Police report?" I asked.

"They are not at liberty to discuss the case as it is still an open investigation,"

"Ah, that makes sense," I added while poking at my salad.

"One of my sources said that you were some sort of Police Consultant?" he asked while also getting his salad ready.

Before answering, I watched as he took most of the toppings off of the salad before adding the dressing that was on the side.

"Who did you hear this from?" I asked.

"I guess it won't hurt to tell you, but it was the receptionist at the Station,"

"She always did like to gossip," I laughed.

"That is great in my profession. It makes getting information easier, rather than going through the trash or anything else gruesome that needs to be done to get the correct information. Is it true that Officer Franks and Officer James are the ones on the case?"

"It is true," I said in between bites.

"So tell me, how did you end up being a Police Consultant?"

"It was from an unfortunate set of circumstances. I was the main suspect in the case. I was cleared, then due to my personal relationship with Officer James, he allowed me to sit in,"

"Personal relationship?"

"I always helped him with his school reports throughout the years. With his personal voucher within the force, I was able to assist on the case,"

"Sounds too good to be true," Alex added.

"It was kind of was, but I'd like to think that I've been a valuable asset in solving the case,"

"The case is solved?"

"Not quite, I've helped the lead detectives in developing a solid theory, and now they won't tell me how they plan to test it,"

"Care to comment on what that is?"

"Not at this time. This is still an active investigation," I added.

"I see,"

The waitress brought our main dish over, and Alex pulled out his cell phone and took a call.

"Excuse me, miss, can I have a to-go box? I've had something come up, and I have to leave,"

She left and returned quickly with his bill and the boxes he would require to take his meal with him.

"Everything alright?" I asked.

"Sorry, source stuff. I'm not at liberty to discuss their personal situation at the moment. It was great talking with you, Lola until we meet again,"

"How are you so sure that we will?"

"I'm not done with you yet," he said as he made his way out of the now-busy restaurant.

I looked around and noticed that there were several families who had come in for their nighttime meal, but they were seated a good distance away from where Alex and I had been. Alex tried to give off an ominous presence, but he did just the opposite. He would almost be considered a brute for his size alone, and his knowledge of certain things put me on edge slightly.

My inner voice couldn't help but wonder if these people knew something that I didn't. Pushing the meeting aside, I finished my meal and paid my bill before heading out into the now-cold night. I glanced at the stars before heading to my car. Once I was ready, I put the car in gear and headed toward home.

Pulling out of the parking lot, I immediately noticed another car behind me. I didn't think anything of it because this was a busy place to eat over the weekend. I began to head toward home, and that was when I noticed that the car behind me had never turned off another road. I quickly decided to head to the Police Station to see if Officer Franks and Officer James would still be in. This was a far-fetched idea, but the car behind me put me on edge.

I pulled into a parking space, and the car behind me did, too. I quickly walked into the Station and headed back toward their desks.

"Excuse me, can I help you?" the receptionist asked.

"I was looking for somebody, and I thought they came in here," a male voice said.

"There was somebody who just came in, but she is here on official business. Is there something that I can assist you with?"

"Can I go back and look for her?"

"Not unless you have business with the Officers,"

"Fine, we'll just wait until she comes back out to her car," the voice said.

"Just great; what kind of situation have you gotten yourself into now?" I said in a low voice.

"Lola?" Mike's voice sounded throughout the bullpen.

"Mike?

"What are you doing here this late? James and Franks have gone home for the night. Is there something I can do to help?"

"This is going to sound strange, but somebody is following me, and I'm afraid to go home by myself. I was going to check in with the guys, but since they have gone home already, I'll just have to brave it," I said half-heartedly.

"We can escort you," Mike offered.

"Really? You don't mind?"

"Not at all. Let me get Sasha, and we'll be ready,"

SEVENTEEN

I was escorted home just like Officer Mike had said. At first, when both of our vehicles had left the parking lot, the third followed, too. It didn't take them long for him to realize that the Police car, which had stayed slightly behind me, wasn't going anywhere. Officer Mike made sure to give me enough space, but I could also tell that he was checking out the car that had followed us from the parking lot. I made quick work to the neighborhood without breaking any laws, and when I pulled into my driveway, I felt safe.

"Did you happen to catch the license plate from the car that had been following you?" Officer Mike asked as he got out of the car to ensure there wasn't any danger lurking around.

"No, I'm sorry. I kind of panicked," I admitted.

"I think Sasha got most of it, I just wanted to compare notes, but we'll run it down and see if anything awry comes up. Just take it easy for the rest of the night. Do you want us to have a patrol swing by later just to make sure everything is okay?"

"If you have extra people and wouldn't mind?"

"I'm pretty sure we can have someone go on a midnight run later. Be careful, and we'll see you later," Officer Mike said.

I waved my goodbyes and headed into the house. Jinx jumped into my arms, and her fur was raised in alarm.

"Jinx? What is it?"

She hissed toward the living room, and I grabbed the ball-bat beside the front door.

"Ms. Lola, you can put the bat down. We're not here to hurt you," a female voice purred.

I walked cautiously into my living room, and there sat a woman whom I had never seen before, but she was gorgeous. She had two henchmen standing off to the side in my dining room, taking up so much space their shoulders were touching one another.

"Who are you, and how did you get into my house?" I asked without stuttering.

I might be sixty-five and just retired, but I played on the local softball team every year. I knew how to swing a bat if need be.

"My name is Eva, and you have something my Boss would like returned," she purred.

"What would I have that somebody would want back?"

"A key,"

I lowered the bat slightly, thinking about her answer. Then raised it again in a defensive position.

"What kind of key?"

"I think you know exactly what key she speaks of," one henchman said.

"Brutus, enough. Lola, I don't really have the time to be bothered by this, but my Boss has asked me to take care of this matter personally. He has you on camera taking something from his safe back at the Bingo Haven. When he inventoried the safe, the only thing he found missing was the key. Now, please hand it over so I can get out of here. I have other issues to attend to tonight," Eva said with a hint of menace in her voice.

"What will happen if I don't give it over willingly?" I asked.

"That is what these men are here for. To ensure that you do hand it over, willingly or not. If need be, they are very good at disposing of bodies. If you catch my drift,"

My eyes went wide at what they were implying. I dug around in my purse, pulled out the key, and handed it over to Eva without any hesitation.

"Here," I said.

"Good. You will not call the Police on this matter. We will be watching Lola," she said as the three of them got up to leave.

I finished lowering the bat and stepped out of the way so they could leave, hopefully without another word.

"Like Eva said, no Police," Brutus whispered on his way out.

I didn't say anything, and even after they left, it took a few minutes for me to register what just happened. I exhaled in relief because my intruders were gone.

I rushed to the window to see how they were leaving, and I saw just in time a large black SUV pull up. Brutus opened the door for Eva to get into the back seat. Somebody was seated in the back with her, but I couldn't tell who it was. The second henchman, who didn't speak, got into the front seat, and Brutus stayed behind. Once the passengers were in the car, it drove off. Within a moment, a second SUV, just like the first, pulled up, and Brutus got into the passenger seat, and it drove off much more slowly.

What was I going to do? Frustrated at my situation, I went to the front door and locked it tight. They must have picked the lock to get in. Maybe I would have to start deadbolting it for extra safety.

I turned off the lights and headed toward the bedroom to get ready for bed. I brought the bat with me for added protection.

That feeling of once being safe was absolutely gone. I had a funny feeling that this wasn't over with in the slightest. I changed into my nighttime clothes and opted for a two-piece long-sleeve and pants outfit.

I had just drifted to sleep when Jinx began to hiss again. I quietly got up and hid behind the dresser, which would hide me from the intruder. There wasn't any light coming in from the moon, nor were there any lights on in the house. It was completely dark.

"Shh, she should be in here," Brutus' voice whispered.

"What are we supposed to do?" another male voice asked.

"You heard the Boss; he wants her out of the picture,"

I was totally screwed. There weren't any phones in my bedroom, and I was going to have to make it to the living room to get my house phone.

My bedroom door began to nudge open, and Jinx hissed at the intruders.

"Shh, little kitty," Brutus said.

I pinned myself as close as I could to the wall and waited for the right moment. It's now or never.

Brutus inched a little closer and flicked on a flashlight. I swung the bat as hard as I could and prayed that it made contact.

Suddenly, there was a loud thud on the floor, and Brutus fell from the momentum of my attack. I rushed over him, and his accomplice tried to stop me. He slammed me into the doorway, almost making me drop the bat, but I held on to it.

He reached for my throat, and there wasn't anything I could do to fight back. I grabbed at his hands, trying to get any extra breath I could, but it was starting to feel useless. The house began to go dark, and with my adrenaline pulsing, I did the only thing I could think of. I began to kick and pray that I did some damage. I was suddenly dropped, and as my body began to intake more oxygen, I ran for the living room and dialed 911.

"911, what's your emergency?" the operator asked.

"There are at least two guys who have broken into my house and have attacked me," I shouted.

"Can you get to a safe place?" the operator asked.

I saw Brutus rush behind me, and he grabbed the phone and threw it against the wall, shattering it.

"The Boss wanted this to be a clean kill, but you have made it a tad bit more difficult," Brutus shouted.

He pulled out a gun, and I dropped the bat entirely to surrender.

"Please, you don't have to do this," I begged.

"I'm afraid I do," Brutus said with an evil smile.

Jinx jumped onto Brutus and scratched at his eyes, and the gun went off. I shouted in pain as a fiery sensation was sent throughout my entire body. I wasn't sure how bad it was, but I couldn't lift my arm. There were a few more gunshots, and then several sparks from deep within the wall lit up the entire room. The sudden smell of something burning filled the air, and then my front door was busted open.

"Freeze, Police!" Officer Mike's voice bellowed through the air.

"There's two of them!" I shouted as the sound of broken glass sounded at the back of the house.

"I'll go around back!" Officer Sasha shouted.

"Lola! Are you hurt?" Officer Mike said as he hauled Brutus to his feet and handcuffed him.

"He fired his gun, and I think I might be hit or just grazed. I'm not sure,"

"Can you get up and walk out..." Officer Mike trailed off.

There was a sudden cracking noise, and then the smoke alarms began to go off,"

"Was there any spark of light anytime during the firing?" Officer Mike asked.

"Yes," I said as smoke began to pore out of every surface.

"Lola, I need you to get out of here now!" Officer Mike shouted as he hauled Brutus away.

I got up from the floor using my good arm and scooped up Jinx along the way.

"Such a good kitty," I said to her.

She purred but only slightly because it was getting harder to see in my smoke-filled home. I rushed out of the house and to my yard, and that was when I saw Jasper's truck pull up. I was still flustered with him, but I was grateful to have a friend around. The other neighbors started to emerge from their homes as well, including my newly found friend Arthur.

"Lola, what happened?" Jasper asked.

"Lola, the paramedics are on their way. So is the fire department. They will be here in just a few minutes to contain the fire that started," Officer Sasha said.

"Fire?" Jasper asked, shocked.

"It's a long story. I would prefer to have my arm looked at first, and then I will tell you the tale of what happened today," I said.

"Lola, are you alright?" Officer Sasha asked.

"I feel faint," I said before trying to take a step away from the house.

I fell to the ground, and I couldn't hear what was going on around me. I heard Jasper trying to say something to me, but it was garbled.

I was being rolled over, and suddenly, my right arm, which was hurt during the shootout, had a breezy feeling.

"What are you doing to her?" Jasper said faintly.

"We have to cut away the clothes to see what we're dealing with," a female voice responded.

Then there was no more noise. I was being lifted up into the air and then hauled away.

"Lola? Can you hear me? You've lost a lot of blood from your wound. I need you to stay awake for me,"

I felt pinching and pressure being tied around my arm, and I would have guessed that someone was trying to place something around it.

"Lola, I need you to listen to me. The gunshot went through and through; you are going to need to ensure it didn't hit anything nerve-wise, but if you can stay awake for me, I'm pretty sure you'll make it through this,"

"So...dizzy..." I managed to croak out.

"That's from the blood loss. Are you on blood thinners?"

"Yes," I whispered.

I forced myself to open my eyes; I wasn't going to go because of blood loss. There were several bumps that caused more pain, but the less I thought about it and used more of my brain power on why this person who, the henchmen called the Boss, wanted me dead.

Maybe I knew who this bad guy was the entire time? What would make somebody think that I was going to be a liability? What if this Mr. Mysterious wanted to twist Jasper's arm and would put him in his place by showing how much of a brute he could be.

This Eva person who was in my house earlier said that the Boss wanted her to personally handle the situation with the key. The way she was dressed was as though it was for some type of gala. I wouldn't have guessed that she would get her hands dirty, but what if she was that kind of player? She couldn't because of where she had to be in a few minutes.

I tried to pull my mind into overdrive, but it was difficult because the ambulance doors burst open, and I was hauled away. Several people were trying to talk to me, but I couldn't make out everything they were trying to tell me.

"Surgery!" Jasper's voice echoed down the hall.

I wasn't sure how he had made it here before the ambulance, but I was glad that he was here nonetheless.

"Lola, I'm going to put a mask on you, and I need you to count back from ten," a male voice said.

"Why?" I asked.

"You need to have surgery so we can figure out why you haven't stopped bleeding yet,"

I tried to fight the mask, but it was no use. The technician held it firm against my face, and I was out.

I AWOKE in the surgery recovery section of the hospital, and there were already a million questions on my tongue.

"Excuse me," I said meekly.

"Oh, you're awake. That's good. Let me tell the Doctor," a nurse said.

I looked around the room and then at my right arm. The wound was on my upper arm, but the bandage covered my shoulder, too.

"Hello? Lola? How do you feel?" a man asked.

"Tired and wondering what happened,"

"You were shot in your home, and then the bleeding wouldn't stop. My head surgeon thought it was best for us to take a look at what was going on under the skin, and boy, was it a good thing that we did. The bullet caused the bone to shatter and fracture into several pieces. One of those tiny pieces cut an artery and wouldn't stop bleeding,"

"How long will I be in recovery?"

"I'd say that we keep you for at least twenty-four hours, and then we can see from there,"

"How long did the surgery take?" I asked.

"Over eight hours, we had to put back together the bone that was shattered. You will be placed into a different recovery room in a few hours, and then you can have visitors,"

"A few hours?"

"We need to ensure that you're stable before we move you. I think you'll be ok, but just to be on the safe side, that's all,"

The Doctor left me alone to my thoughts, and it was the slowest few hours that seemed to pass. I waited patiently as the nurses came by on shifts every fifteen minutes to check my vitals.

"Alright, I gave the Doctor the last of the vital reports, and he wants to move you to another recovery room," a nurse said.

"Do you need me to get into a wheelchair to move?" I asked.

"No need, we will move you via bed,"

A second nurse popped into the area, and both of them navigated the halls to take me up two floors to outpatient recovery.

We passed several other workers along the way, and the two guiding me said their hellos but continued on their path to my assigned room. They wheeled me in and then secured the bed to ensure it wouldn't roll anywhere.

"You already have visitors waiting to see you," one of the nurses said as they both exited the room.

Jasper rushed in first, along with Officer Franks and Officer James.

"What happened?" Jasper asked with flowers in his hands.

"Jeez, Jasper, can't you wait until she is settled. She just came out of surgery not too long ago," Officer James said.

"Lola, I hate to bombard you, but we are here to collect your official statement for the crimes that have been committed against you," Officer Franks said.

"Crimes?" I asked.

"Attempted murder," Officer James added.

I lay in bed, trying to think of everything that had happened several hours before.

"Was there a gala in the area?" I asked.

"What?" Jasper questioned.

"What does having to know about a gala have to do with your accident?" Officer Franks asked.

"Yes, there was," Officer James added.

EIGHTEEN

"Lola, what does that mean?" Jasper asked.

The three of them were waiting for me to answer, but I didn't.

"Has there been a reporter hanging around the Station asking a bunch of questions? He goes by the name of Alex?" I asked, still ignoring their questions.

"No," Officer James answered.

"I guess I better tell you everything that happened," I said.

I started from the beginning and included the fight with Jasper for proper context. Then, ended with the fight that ensued at my house.

"What?" Officer James asked, shocked.

"You don't believe my story?" I asked a little hurt.

"If it was anybody else, I probably wouldn't believe it. Since it's you, I'm surprised you were able to fend off two hulking men," Officer James said.

Officer Frank's cell phone rang, and he excused himself from the room to take the call.

"From what the Doctor told me, I'm probably not going to be able to use a bat again. He didn't go into detail on what they did, but since the bone shattered, I can only imagine what they had to do to fix it," I said sadly.

"No way! You're amazing during the league," Jasper added tenderly.

"Unfortunately, I do have some healing time ahead of me, but what are we going to do about Mr. Mysterious?" I asked.

Officer Franks came back in with a disgruntled look on his face.

"What is it?" Officer James asked.

"That was the fire department. They were able to tell me about the fire that started in your home. It was an electrical fire, and luckily, they were able to put it out before the house was completely gone. However, you won't be able to go home after you leave the Hospital. There is smoke damage done to the entire house. You should get a call from your insurance shortly to start a claim. Until then, what are you going to do for recovery?" Officer Franks asked.

"I guess I'll stay at a hotel for a while, or at least find something I can afford maybe,"

"Of course not! You'll stay with me. What if someone comes back to try and finish the job?"

"What about Jinx?"

"She can stay too, you know she loves me anyway,"

"Ya'know, you left out the part as to why you were asking questions about the gala and the reporter," Officer James added.

I then told them my hunches about Eva and her attire and how I thought she was with Mr. Mysterious.

"That makes sense," Officer Franks said.

"What about this reporter, Alex?" Jasper asked.

I explained in more detail about how Brittany did some digging at the local paper and said her contact who does the hiring hasn't signed on any new reporters.

"Then what paper does Alex work for, and who are his sources that he supposedly has in town?" Jasper asked more to himself rather than the group.

"I have a wild suggestion," I said softly.

The three men quieted down and allowed me a moment to compose myself from the pain that my arm caused.

"What if Alex, the reporter, is Mr. Mysterious?" I said.

Nobody said anything, but each gave me a wild look of their own as though I didn't make any sense.

"Why would you think that?" Officer James asked.

"Doesn't the perpetrator always try to insert themselves into the investigation to see how much the Police have on them?" I asked.

"She does have a point," Officer Franks added.

One of the machines that I was hooked up to started to beep loudly.

"What did you do?" Jasper joked.

A nurse came into the now crowded room and pushed a button on the machine, which caused it to quiet down.

"What did you do?" she joked.

"I haven't moved," I said weakly.

"You need to rest. This has put too much strain on your system, and it needs time to heal. I'm sorry, everybody, but I'm going to have to ask you to leave," the nurse said as she ushered everybody out.

"I'll call to check in on you in a bit, Lola; I'm going to start making arrangements for your recovery," Jasper said a little loudly.

I didn't have the strength to call out to him. Instead, I closed my eyes, which were getting heavier by the second, and allowed sleep to overtake me.

I OPENED my eyes and looked around the dark room. I heard a noise coming from across the room, and I saw the glint from the jewelry on their hands from the hallway's dimmed light.

"How nice of you to wake up," Alex said.

"Who are you?" I croaked.

"I think you've known all along," he mused.

"What do you want with me?" I asked, trying to find the call button for help.

"I see what you're doing, and I've already made sure nobody is going to save you this time," he said menacingly.

"What have I done to you?" I whispered.

"It's your fault. You are the one who is unraveling everything. If it hadn't been for you inserting yourself into the investigation and helping those stupid Officers, they would have never put the dots together,"

Me and my big brain.

"Why did you murder Tom Burchfield?"

"He knew too much, just like you. The only thing with your death, I'm going to make it look like an accident,"

My heart rate picked up, and the machine hooked up to it began to beep loudly in response.

"Now, now. There's no need for that. You might cause the alarm to go off at the nurse's station,"

I couldn't fend for myself and prayed that was exactly what would happen. Alex got up from the seat that he had occupied and slowly made his way toward me. My adrenaline was beginning to surge throughout me, but there was nothing I could do in order to save my own life.

"Is Alex your real name?" I asked.

"Not even close,"

He picked up the IV line and opened the port where medication would have been injected, and, in his other hand, an empty syringe with the plunger pulled back.

"This won't hurt. Or at least that's what I've told the others anyway," he laughed.

The machine that told my heart rate was beeping so loudly I wasn't sure how the nurses hadn't heard it.

"What's going on in here?" a nurse shouted from the doorway.

He tried to hide the empty syringe, but it was too late. The nurse had seen the danger and began to yell.

"SECURITY!"

Alex dropped the IV line and dropped the weapon on the ground in his haste to make it out of the room before he was trapped. I heard him running down the hall, and not long after, the Officers stationed at the Hospital were chasing after him.

"I'll call the Officers who were here earlier. They asked me to tell them if anything new was to come up," she said.

A third guard came to the door, and she left for what I presumed to be an unpleasant phone call. The adrenaline that had been coursing through my veins had no outlet and was starting to make me feel dizzy. I leaned back in the bed, which I also hadn't realized I had sat up from my propped-up position.

"I've heard about you, Ms. Lola, from other guys on the force. They have nothing but good things to say about you," the Officer at the door said.

I looked in his direction and tried to look at him more clearly, but the dizziness hadn't worn off yet. Despite everything that had just happened, I was about to close my eyes when the same nurse entered my room again.

"Lola, your friends are on their way back in. They will be here shortly," she said softly.

I closed my eyes to the world around me and allowed the sounds to lull me into a kind of semi-sleep state.

"Where is she?" Jasper's voice rang through the hall.

"Shh. She has been drifting in and out of sleep since we called you. I've been checking in on her periodically," the nurse said.

"You just called. How could she have been in and out of sleep?" Officer Frank's voice whispered in the doorway.

"I can hear you," I said meekly.

I heard the footsteps of three different individuals enter the room. The overhead light flicked on, and I squinted against the sudden brightness.

"What happened?" Officer James asked.

I steadied my breathing and then told them everything that had happened. I even pointed to the empty syringe that was still on the floor from where he dropped it on his way out.

"You're sure that one of the nurses didn't drop this?" Officer Franks asked while putting on a pair of gloves.

"Positive. It's the kind of thing that you don't miss when someone is trying to kill you," I added.

Jasper stayed silent the entire time but had a look of pure disgust on his face. Officers James and Franks continued to banter me with questions, but nothing unfriendly. They, too, looked genuinely concerned for my well-being.

The three men walked out of the room and conferred with the Officer stationed outside my room. I tried to listen in, but it was useless. Jasper caught me and gently closed the curtain to block my view so I couldn't even try to read their lips.

Who was this Alex person, really?

More thoughts started to swirl around deep inside me when the same nurse from earlier entered the room with the Doctor.

"Lola, are you alright?" he asked.

"As good as I'm going to get, I guess," I replied.

"Did the man who tried to hurt you touch anything in the room?" he asked.

"Yes, the IV tube," I admitted.

"I see. Nurse, please carefully disconnect the IV and get a new one running immediately. I want this one tested for prints," he bellowed.

I couldn't believe that I had forgotten about the part where he tried to insert the empty syringe into the IV.

"Doctor?" I asked.

I guess he was about to turn and head out the door to talk with the others, but he stopped in his tracks and looked back at me.

"Yes?"

"With what Alex was going to do to me, would it have killed me?" I questioned.

"Do you really want me to answer?" he countered.

"You just did," I gulped.

The nurse was still changing out the tubing when he left. She didn't say anything but kept glancing my way.

"Is there something you wanted to ask?" I asked softly.

"I moved here from a larger city hoping to take away the scare of violence around every corner. It's almost been a year being here, and now there have been two attempted murder cases in less than twenty-four hours,"

"What do you mean by two cases?" I questioned.

"There is another patient; he's not from around here. He was in a car accident. His brakes went out, and he swears that it was an attempted murder case. I didn't believe him, but he has proof that he just had his car worked on yesterday. The Officers who were on the floor to question him were down the hall when I yelled out,"

"New to town..." I pondered. "Do you mean Arthur?"

"I can't confirm nor deny any information due to HIPAA reasons," she blushed.

"I need to speak with him," I said, trying to get out of bed.

"I don't think so," she glared.

"Who's to stop me?" I questioned.

"I will. I'll have the Doctor order restraints, and we will keep you in your room," she shouted.

"Do you think that you said it loud enough?"

"What's going on here?" Jasper questioned as he and the two Officers walked back into the room.

"She thinks that she is leaving the room," the nurse commented.

"I don't think so," Jasper chimed in.

"We have all conferred and think it's in Lola's best interest if we move rooms for her safety, along with the other patient who is under investigation. She is to stay in the Hospital for a few days to check on her vitals and try to get everything sorted out on the outside," Officer James said.

"If you have to restrain her, I guess you can do whatever you need to ensure she stays put," Jasper said.

I didn't agree or disagree with their decisions. At the present moment, I haven't been visited by the Arson Detectives or have yet to determine anything from my home.

"Alright, I'll get it updated in the system," the nurse said.

"I don't think that it would be wise to put in the computers. What if that information is compromised?" Officer Franks added.

"You think someone hacked the computers?" the nurse questioned.

"We will have to have a cyber team confirm any suspicions we have, but we can't be too careful. After all this, Mr. Mysterious found Lola's room without disturbing anybody. Who knows how long he was waiting. He could have just done the deed and left," Officer James added.

"Why didn't he?" I spoke up.

"What if he was here on another mission?" Jasper questioned.

"You mean the other patient that was injured?" the nurse asked.

"We'll have to talk with him before we leave," Officer James said.

"I want to come too," I croaked.

"No way," Jasper paused to look at everyone in the room. "I'll stay here with you until things are underway,"

Everybody left except Jasper, who made himself comfortable in a chair seated next to me. He reached for the remote and began to flip through the channels.

"So, what time does breakfast start?" he asked casually.

"What?"

"You know, for food? You have to eat and regain some of the strength you lost. You're not in your roaring twenties, Lola, and it's going to take time to heal from the surgery,"

I sighed in frustration, but he was right. As I've been getting older, it has taken longer for simple cuts and other bumps and bruises to heal.

"You know, not everybody has genetics like myself," Jasper laughed.

I didn't laugh with him; I just waited until he found something to watch on the small TV that was placed in my room.

A few hours had passed with silence between us when there was shouting from the hallway. Lights began to flash blue in another room. I could see the light that spilled into the hallway. The hospital intercom rang out code blue, and then there was a scramble of nurses and others hustled about. I would have assumed a crash cart was being pushed because that was all I heard from the team yelling next to my room.

"What's going on?" I asked.

"It looks like the patient beside you has been put under a code blue," Jasper said.

"Do we know them?" I asked.

Jasper got up from the chair that he had staked as his own and slowly went to the doorway to look around. He shut the door gently and made his way back to the chair.

"Even if we do know them, they deserve privacy at this moment," Jasper said solemnly.

I huffed, but he was right.

"I never could stay out of the gossip world," I laughed.

He laughed, too, knowing it was the truth. I just prayed that everybody in that situation was going to be alright. Shortly after, the blue lights went off, and the Hospital called a code blue cancel. The worst must be over, for now, anyway.

"When do you think they are going to move me?" I asked.

"Hopefully, soon,"

The time came for the breakfast order to be placed, but I wasn't in the mood to eat. Jasper grabbed the menu from one of the counters and looked it over before making a meek face.

"What's that face for?" I asked.

"How is anybody supposed to like the food here?"

"I'm not really hungry," I smiled weakly.

"I figured, but I'm going to order you a fruit plate with some yogurt. That way, you will have to eat something, even if it is small,"

Jasper grabbed the phone that was in the room and ordered some food for me and then something for himself. He asked for a separate tab, and he will pay for it before the end of the day. I'm not sure how he got away with that, but this was a smaller town.

A different nurse knocked on the door before entering and explained that they were finally able to get a new room for me without the computer systems knowing. Jasper explained that we had just ordered breakfast, and she assured us that it would be delivered to the new location.

A few male nurses came in to help move the bed and the equipment that I was still hooked up to, and we easily made our way down the hall.

Jasper stayed behind to talk with a couple of nurses and the Officers who were stationed on this floor.

"Ms. Lola? It's time for us to change the dressings on your arm, and we need to check your vitals and a few other things," the female nurse said.

NINETEEN

My time at the Hospital was finally over, and I hadn't been allowed any visitors other than Jasper, per Officer James and Officer Franks. They insisted it was for my own protection, but it still didn't make me any less grumpy.

Jasper was able to convince the Doctor that I had a place to stay while my house was still under investigation from the electrical fire that had started during my fight with Mr. Mysterious' henchmen. I had been on the phone, and they weren't sure if the house would be repairable. There was so much damage done to the internal structure that it was deemed unsafe. When Jasper drove me to his house, I asked him to drive by mine so I could see it for myself, but he refused, as it would dampen my morale.

This only confused me more because of the way he and Officer James and Officer Franks talked; it was as though my house wasn't even there anymore. According to the arson investigators, there was extreme damage done to the house, and we might have to demolish it.

"Jasper?" I called from his living room.

"Just a moment, I'll be right there!" he shouted from the kitchen.

"I can get up and walk around, you know."

"Let me at least make sure you're comfortable," he chastised.

"It's my arm that was repaired, not my legs. Let me get up and stretch my limbs. If I need help, which I undoubtedly will, I will yell for you. I have to learn to use my arm as is, or it will cease up and not work properly,"

"Yeah, I heard what the Doctor said,"

"You don't have to take care of me like this; I can find another way,"

"Lola, you don't have any children to take care of you, and I'm just a friend who helps out. You can repay the favor one day," he laughed.

Finally able to shoo him away, I got up and stretched my limbs. I looked outside the windows and was slightly startled by the view, but quickly remembered it wasn't my own. Jinx stretched up and rubbed against me and mewed. I bent down carefully and petted her. I wasn't sure how I was ever going to repay Jasper for his act of kindness to Jinx and me.

"Are you expecting anyone?" I called out.

"No,"

I couldn't make out the car until it pulled into his driveway. It was Officer James and Officer Franks. They stepped out of their car and walked up to the door, and rang the doorbell.

"I'll get it," Jasper yelled.

I heard the muffled voices from the doorway, and then all three men were in the living room, which I would call my home for a little while.

"What's wrong?" I asked.

Officer James sighed and put his hands in his pockets. "We figured it would be easier to come from us rather than someone else,"

I couldn't help but look at them skeptically.

"Alex left the country," Officer Franks said.

The news shook me to my core and made me sit down from the shock.

"What can be done?" I asked.

"There's nothing we can do. He's on a watch list, and if he does try to re-enter the country, his passport will be flagged," Officer James said with his gaze averted.

"What are you not telling me?" I asked.

"When we flagged him for attempted murder, there were a few other cases that popped up with similar possible unsolved cases,"

"Let me guess, from the cult case that Molly Kent tried. I gathered the reason Jasper you were running away from her was you were a whistle-blower about the suspicious deaths within the camp?"

"Yes. I was going to tell you, but I didn't want to endanger you," Jasper said.

"Too little, too late," Officer James said, raising his gaze to look me in the eyes.

"What if the person you put away all those years ago wasn't actually the head of the organization?" I questioned.

"What you're asking is impossible," Jasper said in a hushed tone.

I tried to fully grasp what I was trying to say. What if this Alex person was the head of the organization all those years ago? What if he used his minions to take the blame, and he could reinvent himself somewhere else. Why would he need Jasper, though?

"Jasper?" I asked.

"How on Earth did you figure out that I took something?" he asked.

"I've known you for many years. Numbers have always been your thing," I laughed.

"I took the master key along with all of their account information and anything else they would have needed to keep the ruse going," Jasper said.

"What did you do with it?" Officer Franks asked.

"I put it in a safety deposit box several cities over. It's been there ever since,"

"Did you assume a new identity when you left?" Officer James asked.

"No, I didn't think I needed to. I agreed to testify as long as the bad guys were put behind bars," Jasper added.

"What if what Lola is saying is true? That Mr. Mysterious or Alex or whatever he goes by was the true leader of the cult group?" Officer Franks asked.

"They called themselves an activist group back in the day," Jasper blushed.

"Were they a political group?" Officer James asked.

"No, in fact, they always seemed to love bingo," Jasper said.

"Bingo?" Officer Franks asked.

"Yeah. It was always the favorite pastime," Jasper concluded.

"Bingo?" I said to myself.

"Lola? Did you say something?" Officer James asked.

"Oh, it's nothing, just trying to piece together some things," I lied.

I got up to excuse myself and headed into the bathroom, and finished listening to the conversation. They continued to talk about several possibilities of what the next step would be, but I felt that the Officers were not being completely forthcoming.

Maybe I could get in touch with a few of the others on the force and see if they know anything else that's going on.

"That sounds like a plan," Jasper said loudly.

I exited the bathroom, pretending not to have eavesdropped on part of their conversation, but I didn't really hear any good ideas coming from either of them.

The Officers were gone before I was able to say my goodbyes, and Jasper rushed from the door as though he were trying to keep something from me.

"Alright, spit it out," I said.

"There's nothing to tell," he replied, heading to the kitchen.

I didn't want to argue, so I let the subject drop and let my mind wander from place to place. It somehow ended back at the library. I hadn't even been retired for six months, and I was already thinking about going back to work. I mean, I hadn't even seen my house yet, and the therapy that was needed to fully get my arm back in shape to where I could use it again was going to take months.

I made my way over to the couch, which was going to be my makeshift bed for the next several months, and gently tried to lay down without disrupting my arm.

"Here, let me help," Jasper said.

I allowed him to help me get situated, and before he could walk away, I was almost asleep. Jinx jumped on top of me and began to purr so loudly that she drowned out the silence.

I AWOKE, startled, in the middle of the night, with my heart racing and pounding in my ears. It took a moment for me to calm down and realize that I wasn't in my own home. Jinx was still sound asleep on top of me but yawned and stretched from my movements.

The sound of footsteps as they quietly tiptoed around the house caused my adrenaline to spike.

"Hello?" I called out.

The noise stopped in the kitchen, and a light flicked on, revealing a sleepy Jasper.

"Sorry, I didn't mean to wake up. I couldn't sleep and went to get a glass of water," Jasper mumbled.

My heart rate slowed as my body realized that I wasn't in any danger.

"It's ok. I'm just not used to hearing noise at night. I'll adapt," I said as I closed my eyes and waited for sleep to overtake me once again.

THE SUNLIGHT PEEKED through the curtains, which were partially drawn. I stretched, and my shoulder cracked from being stiff all night. My cell phone began to ring, and I didn't recognize the number, but I answered it anyway.

"Hello? Is this Lola?" the voice asked.

"Yes. May I ask who is calling?"

"This is Sean from your insurance company. I was calling because we have an estimate from the damage to your home and how much we will allow for you to rebuild or whatever you plan to do,"

"I see. If the damage is too vast to repair, can I move to another home?"

"Yes,"

"Well, seeing as I haven't been to the house since the incident, I think it would be a good time to do so. How much is the company willing to part with?"

"How about I meet you in person, and we can go over a few details?"

"Fine, I'll be there within the hour. Please don't be late,"

I hung up the phone and went to see if Jasper had awoken for the morning. His door was shut, but there was movement in the kitchen once again. I slowly made my way around to the kitchen to find Jasper had been cooking breakfast.

"Morning," I greeted him.

"I hope you have an appetite," he joked.

"How much are you making?" I laughed.

"Just enough; I'm guessing you need me to take you somewhere?" he said while he flipped an omelet in the pan.

"I need to see the insurance guy who is supposed to meet me at my house in about an hour,"

"We'll eat first, then make our way over there,"

Jasper didn't wait for an answer but began to plate the food that he had been working so hard to prepare. I sat down at his table and waited to be served in silence.

Once he was finished getting everything ready, I waited for him to have a seat, and we both began to eat. Both of us were too busy stuffing our faces for idle conversation. It took me a bit longer to eat since my dominant hand was partially immobilized for the time being.

. . .

JASPER FINISHED QUICKLY and then went to wash the dishes that he had dirtied from making the food. I finished my meal several moments later and then carried my plate to him for cleaning.

"I'll be finished in a few; why don't you go and get ready for the day, and I'll meet you by the door when you're finished,"

I looked down and saw that I was still in some sleeping clothes that were not fit for winter. I made my way to the bathroom and slowly got dressed, really trying to decide if going out was worth it.

After getting ready, I met Jasper by the door, and we walked out toward his truck, which was already warming up. Jasper helped me into the truck, and we slowly made our way toward my house.

"Lola, I don't want this to come as a surprise, but..." he trailed off.

I continued to look in the direction of my home, my brows knitted together in confusion.

"What's this?" I asked.

"This is what's left of your house,"

"I thought there was only smoke damage?"

"No,"

Jasper pulled into the driveway, where my car sat perfectly untouched by the fire.

"There's nothing left," I said sadly.

"I'm so sorry, Lola,"

Another vehicle pulled up to the curb and got out, quickly adjusting his coat to bear against the cold.

"Lola?" he asked.

"Sean, I presume?" I asked.

"Yes. We spoke on the phone not so long ago. As you can see, extensive damage was done to the home. After we reviewed your policy and deemed you fit for coverage, we have agreed to pay out a certain amount,"

He walked over and handed me a piece of paper with a substantial amount listed. I looked back at him, surprised.

"This is what the company thinks my house is worth?" I asked.

"As you can see, there is nothing a construction company can build on. They are going to have to tear down what is left and start over," Sean said.

"That's if I decide to go that route," I added.

"What do you mean?" Jasper asked.

"Yes, you could move to another home and just start fresh," Sean concluded.

I lifted my head high and looked at the rubble that was supposed to be my home.

"Jasper. I might need to stay with you a little while longer if you don't mind?" I asked.

"Stay as long as you need," he said.

"I take it you'll want the funds deposited into your account?" Sean asked.

I shook my head yes and looked at the rubble one more time before turning back toward Jasper's truck. He helped me back inside to the warmth, and then we left.

"Do you want to go anywhere?" Jasper asked quietly.

"I'll be honest. I would love to go somewhere, but I'm so worn out that I would like to head back to your house to rest before therapy in the morning," I said.

TWENTY

Jasper and I had settled into a nice routine, him helping me with my exercises ordered from my physical therapist and other mundane tasks that were still too difficult for me to perform.

I searched every day for a new house to live in, but there was nothing available in the area. I loved this little neighborhood, and the prices were so much cheaper since this was a community for older folks.

I had been sitting in the living room when the doorbell sounded.

"Are you expecting anybody?" Jasper asked.

I shook my head, no, and he got up to answer the door.

"Yes, I was wondering if the lady Lola was here?" the male voice asked.

"She is?"

"You see, I saw her car parked here, and I have been worried about her since the fire,"

"You were at the hospital during the same time Lola was,"

Overhearing their conversation made me antsy, and I couldn't take it anymore.

"Jasper?" I called out.

When I looked around to try and get a better image of who it might be, Arthur walked into the living room.

"Lola! I'm so happy that the bad guy didn't get you," he said with relief.

"Did I hear Jasper correctly? You were in the hospital the same time I was?" I asked.

Jasper had made his way into the living room, too, and took a seat across from me and gestured for Arthur to do the same.

"Yes," he said with a blush.

"What's wrong?" I asked.

"I have to admit there is another reason that I have been looking for you. You see, I think whatever business you have been mixed up with has leaked into my own. I know we have only spoken a couple of times, but I feel that our association has drawn some much-unwanted attention,"

"Oh dear! I'm so sorry that you feel this way. You just moved into the area; what are you going to do?" I asked.

"It's my house, you see. I was hoping that you might have a need for it. It's not set up like yours, but I'm leaving the area. I know your house was burnt to the ground, and since I'm leaving,"

"I hate that our drama has spilled into your lawn..."Jasper started.

"I already have everything worked out with my lawyer and whatnot, you could approach the relator early and maybe strike a good deal?" Arthur suggested.

"Arthur, are you sure about this?" I questioned.

"Absolutely," he beamed.

"When are you leaving?" I asked.

"I'm leaving the state tomorrow. The furniture can stay behind. I'm going to move in with my daughter and have no need for it," Arthur added.

"You mean a fully furnished house, and I might get to stay in the area? This is incredible," I smiled.

"I figured you might like the idea. I'll leave the card so you can call and get something worked out," he winked as he got up from where he was sitting and headed toward the door.

"It was so nice to be friends with you, even for a short amount of time," I added.

"Alas, all good things must come to an end. Take good care of your things and make wonderful memories, for they are all we have in this world. Take care, the both of you," Arthur said.

Jasper escorted him out and came back with a frown on his face.

"What's wrong?" I asked.

"I was getting used to having you around, that's all," Jasper said.

"It will be a little farther than usual, but we can adjust,"

"Yeah, you're right. It will be alright," he added.

I looked at the card that Arthur handed me and wanted to get more information about the house that was going to be for sale. After all, I had a hefty downpayment and could afford the monthly payments for quite some time.

"You might as well call and see what they have to offer," Jasper mused.

I took his advice and headed into the kitchen to make the call. At first, there wasn't an answer, so I left a message and asked for a callback, noting my interest in the upcoming home.

Before I was able to head back into the living room, the phone rang, and it was the realtor's office. Upon answering, we quickly got to business and agreed to meet at the home in a few days to discuss options for home ownership. We ended the call, and I walked back into the living room with a huge smile.

"Good news?" Jasper asked.

"I hope so. We will meet in a few days to discuss the contract and everything else needed. I'm a little nervous; I haven't bought a house in so long," I laughed.

"Ah, it's no big deal,"

The healing process was taking forever on my arm, but at least I didn't have to keep it immobile anymore, and I could now drive myself around town. I was just about to sit down when another call came through on my cell phone.

"Hello?" I answered, walking away from Jasper and the TV.

"Hello, Lola," Alex's voice rang through.

I stopped dead in my tracks, and I felt the color drain from my face.

"Lola, is everything ok?" Jasper asked, worried.

"Wrong number," I said, hanging up the phone.

My phone buzzed from a text message that came through.

Meet me at the Bingo Haven.

I wanted to ignore what it read, but there was this nagging feeling that if I didn't meet up, then there would be chaos still in my life and Jaspers. I got back up and headed to the bathroom, and looked at myself in the mirror. I splashed some cold water onto my face, trying to clear my thoughts. But it was no use.

I wasn't going to live my life in fear anymore. I left the bathroom and readied myself to head to the Bingo Haven. Jasper didn't say anything, just gave me a weird look.

"I'll be back later," I said out loud.

"Drive safe; let me know if you need anything," he responded.

I left the house and made my way to the car. I looked around for Alex's goon squad and, to my surprise, saw nothing on the streets. I went through the motions of driving safely to the Bingo Haven with my thoughts racing. I should have called the Police and told them what was going on. It's too late now.

I pulled into my usual parking spot and slowly got out, not knowing if this was going to be my last time ever seeing this place. I didn't want to think that something bad could happen to me, but then again, my thoughts raced to the murder that had started this fiasco all along.

I stepped away from my car and headed inside. I glanced around and saw that there weren't any other cars in the parking lot. *Great.* As I walked inside, I wasn't greeted by anyone, and the usual busy atmosphere was utterly void of existence, as though there had never been any employees there. The entire building smelled of bleach, and the silence made the hair on the back of my neck stand on end.

"You finally made it," Alex's voice rang through the intercom system.

I walked farther into the lion's den and kept my guard up.

"Aw... I see your all work and no play?"

His voice echoed throughout the building, I continued my path, and he wasn't anywhere to be found. A sudden idea popped into my head as to where he could be. The office.

Slowly, I dragged my feet toward the stairway that would undoubtedly lead to my doom. One by one, I picked them up and made them go down the hallway. The closer I got to the office, I was able to see the door was propped open.

"You don't have to be shy," he cooed.

I really wish I had contacted Officer James and Officer Franks about what I was doing. I wasn't entirely sure what I was doing. As I walked into the office, there sat a shiny silver gun on the desk.

"How nice of you to finally join me. I was starting to get lonely," he smiled.

I looked around the office, and it looked the same as when Jasper and I had broken in.

"What do you want with me?" I asked in a soft voice, shocked to call it my own.

"I want to get rid of you and be free of this wretched town. I think I've worn out my welcome here,"

"It was your own fault, you know," I said.

"What is?"

"You murdered Tom and started this entire investigation,"

"Ah, yes. Tom. He would have made a fine business partner, but he knew too much and declined my advances toward a partnership,"

"So that made you have to kill him?"

"Like I said, he knew too much and had to be dealt with,"

"You killed him yourself, didn't you?" I asked, shocked.

"Sometimes you have to get your hands dirty if you want something done the right way," he said, picking up the gun.

"That's a bit cliché, don't you think?" I asked.

I glanced over at the monitor that was on his desk and saw movement through the front doors. I didn't dare to steal too many glances because I didn't want him to take the chance of him noticing the disturbance. He might act wildly and start to shoot blindly at everything. I knew I couldn't outrun bullets, but maybe I could buy whoever had walked in some time.

"I have a plane to catch that will take me out of the country, and your friend Jasper is going to go with me. Whether he likes it or not," Alex said, glancing at the monitor.

Thank goodness there wasn't anybody there when he looked over.

"What makes you think he will go willingly?" I challenged him, beginning to walk away from the doorway and slowly making my way to a seat.

Alex cocked an eyebrow but smiled more to himself rather than at me. He didn't miss a beat and followed my movements with his gun.

"Who said he had to go willingly?"

Nobody was at the door yet to rescue me, so I had to keep stalling.

"You're going to kidnap him?" I laughed.

"I don't see what's so funny. I'm the one who holds all the power here," he said haughtily.

"Alex, this is the Police; why don't you let Lola go, and we can talk some things through," Officer James' voice bellowed in the hallway.

He looked at the doorway, quickly stood up, and crossed the room to where I was in no time. He pulled me up and began to use me as a human shield.

"There's nowhere to go," Officer Franks said.

"I've got all the leverage I need. I've got hostages, and you will meet my demands,"

"Do you mean Jasper? We know he's not in there with you," Officer James said.

"Of course not," Alex said sheepishly.

"Who else is in the room?" Officer James asked.

"Why don't you come in and find out," Alex said, taking the gun off me and pointing it at the doorway.

"Can't do that, Alex. Too risky for all of us," Officer James said.

I heard thunderous footsteps from down the hall. I was too scared to move, afraid that Alex would actually do the deed that he set out for.

"Did you tell them you were going to meet me here?" Alex whispered into my ear.

I shook my head, no, but he grabbed my good shoulder and pressed farther into the room.

"If you're wondering how we knew to come here, it wasn't because of Lola," Officer James said.

"There's no way somebody turned on me," Alex said to himself.

"Are you so sure about that?" I said in a small voice.

"Do you want me to give you a hint?" Officer James asked.

"I'll bite. How did you know to come to Lola's rescue?" Alex asked.

"It was Jasper. He called us the moment she left and told us something was up. We were able to track her down via cell phone and knew we had to get here," Officer James said.

"How did you get back up here so fast?" Alex said more to himself.

"That would be instinct," Officer James added.

I tried to slowly move away from Alex's piercing grasp, but the more I seemed to fidget, the more he seemed to hold on for dear life.

"Also, we sent some guys over to Jasper's house to make sure nothing funny was going to happen to him. To our surprise, there were three goons sitting right in front of his house as though they were waiting for something or someone to give them orders,"

Alex didn't say anything, as his master plan had just fallen apart.

How was he supposed to get out of here and take Jasper with him? There was only one thing for him to do. Surrender.

"I guess this is the part you want me to surrender?" Alex said, gripping me tighter.

I was getting more nervous by the second. The metal of the gun barrel touched my face, making me uneasy. Alex glanced around the room and began to back up to a window. I tried to peek over at it, but I only saw a partial view of a fire escape.

The window in which he was wanting to escape was partially open already. I never noticed it before, but all he would have to do is finish shoving it the rest of the way open, and then he would be free. Panic began to settle in, and I didn't know what to do.

Suddenly, Officer James stepped into the doorway with his gun drawn and aimed at Alex.

"I wouldn't do that if I were you," Officer James said.

Alex jumped at the sudden movements and pointed the barrel of the gun into my face.

"Don't come any closer," Alex said with a shaky breath.

"I can see that you're thinking of taking the fire escape. I would advise against it," Officer James said.

Alex didn't say anything, just shoved me forward, and Officer James caught me. I turned around to see what was going to happen next, and to my surprise, nobody was going after him. Alex had opened the window all the way and practically fell out of the opening.

"You're going to let him get away?" I asked, shocked.

"Drop the weapon and put your hands in the air!" Officer Franks shouted.

"I told him not to go that way," Officer James said, holstering his gun.

A few moments of silence crept between us, and Officer James didn't say anything as he led me out of the office. We slowly began to make our way toward the center playing area.

"What's going to happen to this place now?" I asked.

"It will need a new owner for sure," Officer James laughed.

"Oh no! Not me. I'm too old to run a business," I joked.

"What about me?" Jasper questioned as he walked toward us.

"How did you know something was wrong?" I asked.

"The way you said bye," Jasper smiled.

"Well, whatever it was, I'm glad that you did what you did. What will happen now? He confessed to murdering Tom and I'll bet he also killed the other person in the warehouse fire." I said.

"Since it was an untaped confession, we will have to try to have him confess it in interrogation," Officer James said.

He walked away and gave Jasper and me some privacy. I looked around the business and sighed out of sadness.

"What's wrong?" Jasper asked.

"I'm going to miss this place. With the investigation still going on, I wonder if Victoria's place will be shut down, too,"

"I guess only time will tell," Jasper added.

Both of us waited for some time for Officer James and Officer Franks to return and ask us questions. They soon released us but advised us not to go out of town. We nodded our agreement and then headed back to Jasper's house.

No sooner than we both walked through the door, Jinx greeted both of us as though she had been worried.

"Jasper, I don't mean to be rude, as you have been a gracious host for allowing Jinx and me to stay here..." I started.

"Lola, don't worry about it. I understand wanting your own space, and I don't blame you for wanting to leave as soon as you can," he smiled.

"I'm so glad that we have been friends all this time,"

"We are still going to be friends, even after all of this," Jasper said confidently.

"Of course we are,"

"You never know; I might be the next owner of the Bingo Haven once all of this is sorted out,"

ABOUT THE AUTHOR

Kevin Dog has loved spinning a tale based on science fiction since he was eight years old. As he grew older, he learned to love other genres and has now begun to write them as well.

When not writing or reading his own works, he loves to learn about the past. He can't help but dive into the worlds of our past and learn everything there is to know so he can find new inspiration for upcoming books.

www.ingramcontent.com/pod-product-compliance
Lightning Source LLC
Chambersburg PA
CBHW070628310726
48982CB00001B/207